CHAPTER ONE

'Philip, I promise you I have had enough adventuring. When a man reaches thirty it is time he took a wife and settled down.'

Major Lagallan exchanged a laughing glance with his own dear spouse, and Mrs Lagallan shook her head at her brother-in-law.

'Vivyan, I do not believe you are serious!'

Mr Lagallan grinned across the dining-table. 'For shame, Caro. I thought you at least would applaud my intention!'

'If you are truly sincere in your wish to marry, I am glad of it. But tell me a little about the woman who has affected this change in you.'

'She was the toast of London last season: Helen Pensford.'

Mrs Lagallan frowned. 'I have never met her, I think. You must remember, Viv, that we did not come to London last year, what with little Philip coming down with chicken-pox, and then Charles had that dreadful cough. When the doctor suggested a little sea air would be beneficial, I took both boys to Worthing. But tell me about Miss Pensford. Is she truly a beauty?'

'Oh, a veritable diamond.' Vivyan Lagallan lifted his wine glass and stared thoughtfully at the dark contents. 'Her breeding is

1

impeccable. The Pensfords own a considerable estate at Combe Charlton, near Bath. Helen is their only child. Very little wit, but she dances like an angel.'

'Oh dear.'

He laughed at the look of dismay upon his sister-in-law's countenance. 'What! Are you jealous, Caro?'

The lady's eyes twinkled.

'Not a bit, you know I made my choice years ago, and have never regretted it!' She reached out a hand to her husband, who caught her fingers and carried them to his lips. She smiled, and continued, 'No, Viv, what I fear is that Miss Pensford sounds far too dull for you. Pray do not laugh at me, I am serious! You have lived all your life for adventure and excitement, and I do not care how beautiful the girl may be, if she is a ninny-hammer she will bore you within a month.'

'Well, I hope you are wrong.' Vivyan refilled his glass and sat back, a faint smile playing about his lips. 'I am travelling into Somerset tomorrow to propose to the lady!'

She bit her lip, frowning at him. 'I hope you will not regret it, my dear!'

*   *   *

Vivyan recalled his sister-in-law's words as his travelling-chariot pulled away from Combe Charlton a week later. Perhaps Caroline was

THE DREAM CHASERS

Melinda Hammond

CHIVERS
THORNDIKE

This Large Print book is published by BBC Audiobooks Ltd, Bath, England and by Thorndike Press®, Waterville, Maine, USA.

Published in 2004 in the U.K. by arrangement with the Robert Hale Limited.

Published in 2004 in the U.S. by arrangement with Robert Hale Limited.

U.K. Hardcover ISBN 0–7540–9665–3 (Chivers Large Print)
U.K. Softcover   ISBN 0–7540–9666–1 (Camden Large Print)
U.S. Softcover   ISBN 0–7862–6490–X (General)

The text of this Large Print edition is unabridged.
Other aspects of the book may vary from the original edition.

Set in 16 pt. New Times Roman.

Printed in Great Britain on acid-free paper.

British Library Cataloguing in Publication Data available

Library of Congress Control Number: 2004101135

right: having spent only a few days in Miss Pensford's company, he was inordinately relieved to get away. The visit had gone exactly as planned: the lady's family had made him welcome, gratified that he had taken up their invitation to take pot-luck with them. His proposal had been accepted, if not with rapturous delight then with satisfaction, and the fact that he had spent the past decade living abroad was easily forgotten when put against his considerable fortune. A family bereavement kept the Pensfords in Somerset, but they promised to travel to London later in the season, and it was agreed that no official announcement should be made until then. Vivyan gazed out of the carriage, and as the pale April sun disappeared behind a bank of trees that bordered the road, he wondered if he had made the greatest mistake of his life.

*   *   *

His reverie was cut short when the carriage lurched suddenly and came to a stand amidst shouts from the coachman and much blowing and stamping from the team of high-bred bays. Mr Lagallan jumped down from the carriage to enquire the cause of their delay, and the coachman touched his hat to him.

'A bag, sir. Someone threw a bag into the road—made the leaders shy, and no wonder!'

Following the coachman's outstretched

finger, Vivyan spotted a large portmanteau lying at the edge of the road. Walking up to it, he pushed it gently with the toe of one of his shiny Hessians.

'Now how the devil did that get there?'

'It is mine.'

Mr Lagallan looked around.

'Up here! In the tree.'

Looking up, Vivyan saw a ginger-haired figure, dressed in a brown woollen suit, gazing down at him through the branches.

'Well now, lad. What do you mean, to be frightening my horses so?' he demanded.

'Please accept my apologies for that, sir. I did not mean it to happen. You see, I scrambled up here to avoid a group of drunken men who were on the highway. I was about to climb down again, when I heard your carriage and thought I had best wait until you had gone by, but my bag slipped down out of my grasp.'

'Well, I think you had better slip down, too,' remarked Vivyan. 'The coast is clear now.'

'That's just it,' said the youth. 'I fear I am stuck. You see, I have been here for so long that I've grown very stiff, and I don't think I *can* climb down.'

Vivyan laughed. 'Well, you don't look too heavy. Lower yourself off that branch, boy, and I will catch you.'

Looking very relieved, the lad swung down from his perch and dropped into Vivyan's arms. He caught the boy easily, and found himself looking down into a pair of clear green eyes. Without releasing his grip, he observed the red hair, scraped back from a wide brow and confined at the neck with a ribbon, and the clear skin with a sprinkling of freckles on a straight little nose. Mr Lagallan's dark eyes gleamed.

'Damme, you are not a boy at all!' he exclaimed, a laugh in his voice. 'I think you must be a wood nymph!'

The body in his arms wriggled to free itself but his grip tightened.

'Oh, no! I shall only let you go if you promise not to run away. I want to know what you are doing alone on the highway, dressed in those clothes.' There was no reply. Vivyan said cheerfully, 'Come now, Miss, you owe me that much for rescuing you.'

The green eyes flashed. 'You did *not* rescue me!'

'Oh? And how else were you going to get down from that tree?' This drew a reluctant twinkle from those engaging eyes, and Vivyan gave her his most charming smile. 'Let us agree that I *assisted* you! Now, nymph, will you promise?'

'Oh, very well.'

He set the girl on her feet, and she stepped back a pace to straighten her rough clothes, saying as she did so, 'Thank you. I am on my way to Bath to catch the night mail to London.

I thought it would be safer to travel as a boy, but when I saw that group of men approaching, I thought it best to hide in the tree until they had passed.'

'Very wise,' said Vivyan gravely.

'Yes, but they did not pass by! They decided to rest on this very spot, and I was obliged to remain in the tree for *hours*! They were only just out of sight when you came by. Perhaps you saw them on the road?'

'Sadly, no. I was—er—sleeping, until your bag dropped from the tree.'

'I am so sorry about that! And I am truly grateful for your assistance, sir, but if you will excuse me, I must press on if I am to reach Bath today.'

Reason told Mr Lagallan that a sensible man would bid this young person adieu and be on his way. But Vivyan had never claimed to be sensible.

'I am myself going that way—perhaps I could take you up as far as Bath?' he smiled at her doubtful glance. 'I promise you will be quite safe: I always travel with a pair of loaded carriage-pistols—look, you could reach one easily if you need to defend yourself.'

An answering smile gleamed in her own eyes. 'Thank you sir, but I doubt that would be necessary.'

'Well, on a more practical level, there is a rug . . . and a hot brick for your feet, if you would like it.'

6

The temptation proved too great. The girl nodded.

'Thank you. You are very kind. I do feel quite chilled, after sitting still for so long.'

Mr Lagallan picked up the portmanteau and tossed it to his footman, then after a word to his coachman, he handed the girl into the carriage.

Warming her toes on the hot brick, and with the travelling-rug tucked about her legs, his companion gave a sigh of contentment.

'That is so very comfortable! Thank you.'

'Think nothing of it. But if we are to be travelling-companions, should we not introduce ourselves? My name is Lagallan.'

'How do you do? I am Eustacia Marchant.'

Vivyan's lips twitched at the absurd formality, but he asked soberly, 'And how comes it that you are travelling alone to London, Miss Eustacia Marchant?'

'I am going to be married!' She saw his look of surprise, and a dark flush crept into her cheeks.

'I am going to find Rupert Alleyne. We fell in love during last autumn, when he was staying with his uncle, near Charlton Temple.'

Mr Lagallan remained admirably serious at this matter-of-fact statement.

'And does Mr Alleyne know you are coming to see him?'

'No, but it is imperative that I find him, before he proposes to someone else!'

'And—er—is he likely to do so? If he loves you, that is.'

'He *does* love me, very much, but Aunt Jayne says his parents are arranging an—an advantageous alliance for him. But if he loves me, I do not see that he should marry anyone else, do you? And it is not as if I am a pauper,' continued Miss Marchant, considering the matter. 'When I am five and twenty I shall inherit my mother's property, and of course there is grandfather's fortune, too, when he dies—Oh!' Her hands flew to her mouth, and her eyes danced as she looked at Vivyan, sitting opposite her. 'That sounds very heartless, but indeed I am very fond of Grandpapa, and have lived very happily with him for years—in fact, I can remember no other home, for my parents died when I was a baby.'

'And how old are you now?'

'I have just turned one and twenty. I know that I look much younger than that,' she added confidentially. 'I was presented two seasons ago, and it was *not* a success. I think I was far too young, then, but Aunt Jayne says she is already much distracted by the arrangements for my cousin Cordelia's wedding and cannot bother with me again until that is over, and Grandfather is far too old to travel to London, so there is no one to come with me, and I *must* find Rupert before it is too late!'

'And you have not seen—er—Rupert since

last year?'

'No. He left Somerset in September, and Mrs Alleyne—his aunt, you know—had a letter from him at Christmas explaining that he was obliged to remain with his papa. So I quite see that he could not come back *then,* but now Mrs Alleyne is hinting that he is looking about him for a rich wife, and I *cannot* let that happen!'

'But, forgive me—I know I must seem very dull-witted—why should—er—Rupert marry someone else if he loves you?'

'Aunt Jayne says he will do so to please his papa, but surely, if I go to London and we explain to Mr Alleyne, he must see that we truly love each other?'

The green eyes were turned trustingly upon Vivyan and he hesitated before making a reply. How could he explain to this absurd child that the young man had most likely looked upon their romance as nothing more than a mild flirtation to pass the time?

He said gently, 'Miss Marchant, let me advise you to go home. I will happily break my journey to take you there myself, and if you like I will carry a letter to young Mr Alleyne. I cannot believe that he would want you to be travelling the country in this way.'

The young lady's countenance took on a stubborn look.

'No, you are very kind, sir, but I *must* find him. You see, I very much fear that if I do not see him and talk to him myself, he will be persuaded to sacrifice himself in marriage to an heiress.'

'But surely your family will be missing you: you cannot wish to alarm them.'

Her sunny smile dawned again.

'No indeed, but they will not worry, for they think I am staying with my old governess! I persuaded Miss Frobisher to invite me to stay for a few weeks. Since she lives but five miles from Bath, I knew I could easily walk there to catch the mail.'

'Do you mean to tell me the lady is a party to your madcap scheme?'

'Oh yes, for she quite sees that one must make a push to secure one's happiness. Besides, I knew she would be able to fit me out with a boy's suit, for she has several nephews, all of whom come to stay with her at times.'

Vivyan dropped his head in his hands.

'Miss Marchant, you are incorrigible!'

'Thank you.'

It was not a compliment!'

'But you do see that I am determined to get to London and find Rupert? If he should marry someone else, it would be the end of all my dreams!' She glanced out of the window. 'Goodness, we have reached Bath already! I am deeply grateful to you, sir, for I was very much afraid that the delay on the road would mean I would be walking into Bath in the dark.'

Gazing down into Eustacia's trusting face, Mr Lagallan realized the impossibility of dropping the child at The White Hart and leaving her to make her own way to London.

'Miss Marchant, if I may make a suggestion? Even in that disguise I cannot think it wise for you to travel alone. The dangers awaiting such an innocent as yourself are legion. I am even now on my way to Town, and if you will not allow me to escort you home, which is the course of action I would most strongly advise, then I would rather take you with me than let you jaunter about the country unattended.'

After only the briefest pause Miss Marchant said, 'Would you indeed, sir? That is excessively kind of you—and a great relief, too, for I have never travelled by mail-coach before, and although I am sure it is very exciting, I have never purchased tickets, or paid vails on the road, and I was not at all sure how I would go on.'

Vivyan gave orders for the coach to continue on to Marlborough and sat back in his corner, realizing with a wry inward smile that he was now committed to a most reprehensible course of action.

*   *   *

His companion, however, had no such qualms and appeared to be in the very best of spirits, chattering away as if they were old friends. By the time they reached Marlborough, he had learned that Miss Marchant lived with her grandfather and widowed aunt near Radstock. The preparations for her cousin's forthcoming nuptials seemed to have been consuming all the family's attention for several months, and it appeared to Vivyan that Miss Marchant had been left to amuse herself during the previous summer. Her innocent remarks only reinforced his suspicion that Rupert Alleyne had whiled away an enforced retirement to the country with a flirtation that had left the young lady desperately in love.

'We must decide what I am going to call you, if you are to continue with your disguise,' said Mr Lagallan as they drove into the inn-yard.

Miss Marchant wrinkled her nose.

'Well, at home everyone calls me Stacey. Will that do?'

'Excellent. The landlord here knows me, so we must pass you off as some sort of cousin. You had best call me Vivyan, at least when we are in company.'

The landlord ushered them into a private parlour, where a cheerful fire had been prepared, and while a serving-maid laid out a substantial supper, Mr Lagallan demanded two rooms for the night. The landlord's tentative suggestion that they should share a room, since the inn was quite full, he quelled with a haughty stare, afterwards turning his stern gaze upon Miss Marchant, who had subsided into giggles as the door closed upon their host.

'The poor man thinks you are very high in the instep! He will have to turn away trade, you know.'

'He will be amply rewarded for his trouble.'

'Oh!' Eustacia reached into her pocket and brought forth a small purse.

Vivyan frowned. 'That was not meant as a cut at you.'

'No indeed, but I cannot let you pay for me.' She held out a handful of coins. 'You will take it, please, sir. I will not be beholden to you!' She smiled as he took the money. 'There, we can be friends again! Shall we have supper now?' She walked towards the little table, where their meal had been laid out.

They sat down to a supper of hashed venison, potted trout and cold ham, finished off with cheese and melon.

'Have you been visiting friends in Somerset, sir?' said Miss Marchant, feeling that conversation was required.

'Something of the sort.'

It is a very fine county; I am told the sport is excellent.'

'Very likely, but I saw little of it at Combe Charlton.'

Miss Marchant's company manners deserted her. She stared at him.

'Combe Charlton? Are *you* the beau who came to propose to Helen?'

Vivyan's brows snapped together. 'I was invited to join the family for a few days.'

'I am sorry if I have offended you, but the Pensfords are our neighbours, and it was common knowledge that Helen had caught—I mean—'

'You know Miss Pensford well?' asked Vivyan, ignoring her discomfiture.

'We have known each other since we were in the school-room. Aunt Jayne was quite determined that I should be presented before Helen, for she said I would be quite over-shadowed by her, and she is right, of course. Helen is very beautiful. Quite empty-headed, but a man does not want a clever wife, Aunt Jayne says.'

'Aunt Jayne could be wrong.'

'But she isn't, is she? You have offered for Helen!'

Mr Lagallan found himself at a stand, and turned the conversation into safer channels. Eustacia followed his lead and chattered away merrily, but when she glanced up some time later she found that Vivyan had stopped eating and was watching her, a slight smile curling his lips. She raised her brows at him, tilting her head to one side.

'Why do you look thus at me, sir?'

'I was thinking how few women of my acquaintance would be so unconcerned, dining

14

alone with me, and wearing a man's clothing, no less!'

Miss Marchant flushed and a slight frown clouded her eyes. 'You must think I am very forward, but when one is in love it makes one act rashly.'

'Imprudently, at all events,' he murmured.

She hung her head, saying in a small voice, 'I suppose it *was* imprudent of me.'

'I was not thinking of you, child.' He rose and held out his hand to her. 'Come, Stacey. Let us take our coffee by the fire.'

*   *   *

After supper, Mr Lagallan escorted his young charge to her room. He urged her to lock her door, hinting at pickpockets and night thieves, and waited in the corridor until he had heard the reassuring click of the lock before making his way to his own bedchamber.

CHAPTER TWO

The next morning they made an early start, for Mr Lagallan hoped to reach London without a second overnight stop. A flock of geese on the road at Froxfield held them up for a while, but after that they picked up speed and Vivyan remarked to his companion that they should

15

be in Town by the evening. He received no reply and looked down at his companion: Miss Marchant was staring silently out of the window.

'This is not like you, Miss Marchant, to be so quiet.'

'No, I am sorry. It is just that I have been wondering what to do when I get to London. I can hardly arrive at Rupert's door dressed this way.'

Mr Lagallan's lips twitched. 'You think Mr Alleyne would not approve of your apparel?'

'Oh, I am sure he would understand, once it was explained to him, but it would be very difficult to keep it from the servants, and just think of the scandal—and I am sorry if you consider that a cause for laughter!'

'No, of course it isn't.' Mr Lagallan made a heroic attempt to look serious. 'I quite see your dilemma. Let us think what we can do. Is there no one else you know in Town who would help you, no aunts or cousins?'

'No one. Except my godmother, Lady Bilderston.'

'A godmother? Well, that is excellent news.'

'Oh no it isn't,' came the damping reply. 'I have never seen her—at least, I suppose she saw *me,* as a baby, when Mama was alive, but all I know of her is that she sends me little gifts on my birthday. She has never made the least push to enquire after me.'

'But you know she lives in Town?'

'Yes, for I am obliged to write to thank her for her gifts, and her direction has never changed—Fanshawe Gardens.'

'A fashionable area, certainly. I feel sure she will not fail to help you.' He found himself subjected to a glance that held more than a hint of doubt and he flicked her cheek with one finger. 'Don't look so anxious, nymph! I'll tell you what we will do: my brother and his wife are in town, in Bruton Street. We will go there first. My sister-in-law will be delighted to help us.'

Eustacia brightened. 'Truly? She will not think it odd that I—that you and I—' She trailed off, colouring.

Vivyan considered how he would explain to Caroline that he had carried out his intention of proposing to one young lady, but had brought another back to London with him. His eyes danced.

'Lord, no,' he said cheerfully. 'Caroline knows me too well to think there is anything odd in this caper!'

Her mind set at rest, Miss Marchant could continue her journey in comfort and she was soon asking Vivyan if they would stop for lunch.

'I quite understand that you do not want me to leave the coach when we change horses, but I am *very* hungry'

'Poor nymph, it is unkind of me to keep you cooped up for so long! But I am planning to stop at Reading, at The Star. They keep a very good table, as well as some excellent brandy!' Eustacia noted the twinkle in his dark eyes, but he merely continued: 'We will take an early lunch there, but we must not tarry: I want to reach London before dark.'

*   *   *

Miss Marchant surveyed the remains of their substantial lunch—boiled fowl, roast partridge and potted char had been provided, together with tarts, cheese and pickles.

'That was delicious!' she declared, when she had tried every dish. 'How much do I owe you, sir?'

Mr Lagallan waved a hand. 'It is my treat, Stacey, as long as you will pour the coffee.'

Miss Marchant thanked him prettily and picked up the coffee-pot. She was determined that he should not pay for her accommodation on the road, but she reasoned that there could be no objection to accepting lunch from him. Hers was a sunny nature, and she had quickly responded to Vivyan's natural charm: she considered him now as a good friend and stood upon the easiest of terms with him. She was well aware that his dark good looks and rakish air might make him a dangerous companion for a young woman, but she knew herself to be in love with Mr Alleyne. Mr Lagallan treated her with a friendly

18

camaraderie that she was able to respond to in the friendliest way, knowing herself to be in no danger of succumbing to his obvious charms. She looked up to find him watching her.

'Why do you look at me, sir?' she said, her head on one side.

'Merely that you seem to be enjoying yourself.'

'Oh, I am! This is my first adventure, and I am enjoying myself immensely.' She added shyly, 'I do not think I should have found it half so entertaining if I had not met you, sir. I have to thank you for taking such good care of me.'

'I cannot think of many who would agree with you! Your relatives would say that I should have returned you to your home immediately.'

The landlord scratched upon the door. 'Beggin' your pardon, sir. Your coachman asked me to tell you that the carriage is ready.'

Mr Lagallan nodded. 'Tell him we will be with him directly.' He looked at his companion. 'Come, it is time to be on our way.'

Eustacia went before him into the passage, where she almost collided with a gentleman in an open boxcoat, entering the inn. With a word of apology she stepped aside, but the gentleman had stopped and was staring at Mr Lagallan. He pushed his curly-brimmed beaver hat back on his fair head and grinned.

'Viv! Viv Lagallan! As I live and breathe, how do you do, sir?'

'How do you do, Nathan?'

'Well, well—are you here on business?'

'On my way to London, as a matter of fact—escorting my young cousin,' he added, as the gentleman's grey eyes rested thoughtfully upon Stacey.

'Cousin, eh? Pleased to meet you, young sir. Nathan MacCauley's the name, and I'm a friend of your cousin—a very old friend, eh, Viv?' He turned his wide smile back upon Vivyan. 'And this is very well met, Lagallan! A word with you, before you go, sir.'

Vivyan nodded at Miss Marchant.

'Pray get in the coach, Stacey. Check that the luggage is loaded, and tell my man to walk the horses.' He watched her move away before turning again to the gentleman beside him.

'Well, MacCauley? As you can see, my team is waiting. I can give you but a moment.'

'Yes, yes, I understand. Let us step into the parlour . . . Ah, you did not finish the coffee. May I?'

'As you wish.' Vivyan perched himself on the edge of the table, one booted leg swinging gently. 'What are you doing in England? The last time we met you were running a snug little gaming hell in Rome.'

'And so I was, Vivyan, my friend, but the dibs weren't quite in tune, and things became a trifle . . . uncomfortable.'

'Ran out of money, did you? That doesn't surprise me—I remember that high-flyer you had living under your protection.'

Mr MacCauley looked hurt.

'Ah, yes. Celestine. I admit to you, my friend, I was taken in there. Damned disappointing, I must say. She was not at all grateful, and when I think of all the money I spent on her! But let's not dwell on that. Do you remember how we travelled through France together, living on our wits? Those were happy days, Viv.'

'Happy? Plunging from one scrape to another?' exclaimed Mr Lagallan. He gave a reluctant grin. 'There was no time for boredom, certainly! But that don't explain why you have returned to England.'

MacCauley refilled his coffee-cup.

'An uncle of mine has died and left me a little money, so I thought I might set myself up in London. Turn respectable, like yourself.'

Vivyan laughed. 'Heaven help us!'

MacCauley grinned. 'I know, the world's turned on its head, ain't it? But it's true. I've a mind to give up this adventuring, but first there's a few matters of—ah—business to tidy up.'

'Such as supplying a little smuggled brandy to this inn?'

Nathan MacCauley looked affronted. 'I gave up that line of business when you did, my friend! No, the rooms are very reasonable here, and most suited to a gentleman like myself. And it's convenient for what I have to do. Once I've concluded my business here, I shall go to Town and live like a gentleman, mayhap even find me a rich little wife.'

Mr Lagallan's lip curled. 'I'd like to see it!'

'That's why I'm so glad I ran into you. You could help me, my friend: introduce me to your circle.'

'I hardly think so!' laughed Vivyan, rising. 'My friends are no pigeons for your plucking, Nathan.'

'But I am a reformed man!'

'Give me proof of your—ah—reformation for the next twelve months and we'll talk again. Until then, goodbye, MacCauley.'

*   *   *

Miss Marchant was almost bursting with curiosity when Vivyan finally climbed into the coach.

'Who was that man?' she demanded as the carriage clattered out of the yard. 'You did not seem very pleased to meet him.'

'I was not. I wanted to get you safely to London without meeting anyone I know.'

'Oh yes, of course. But is he a good friend?'

'Let us say that I knew him in my less reputable days.' He glanced down to find Eustacia regarding him with wide eyes, and he laughed. 'Many years ago I fell in with a group of free-traders—smugglers, my dear! Nathan MacCauley was one of them.'

'Really? He does not look like a villain.'

'Oh, he was born the son of a gentleman, but he's a rogue. He's not above a little thieving and smuggling, but he's a gambler, too: lives on his wits.'

But Stacey had lost interest in Mr MacCauley.

'You were a smuggler?' she breathed, eyes sparkling.

'Not really. I helped them with a couple of runs, but that is all.'

'But how? How did you meet them?'

'It is an unedifying story, nymph.'

He felt a small hand slip into his own.

'Of course I will not press you, but if you would *like* to tell me . . .'

Vivyan found he was not proof against her wistful tone. He settled back in the corner of the coach.

'It was some . . . eight years ago. I was driving on the beach at Sandburrows—do you know it? A little village not a day's ride from Radstock. The beach there is long and smooth, ideal for carriages. I was racing the tide. A foolhardy sport, and it almost cost me my life—and that of a very dear friend. We were cut off by the spring tide. I managed to set the horses free, and they escaped, but I was washed out to sea, clinging to the wreckage of my carriage. I managed to swim to the island of Steep Holm, where I was discovered by a group of free-traders, sheltering in one of the coves. Doubtless I would have died of the cold if they had not stripped me of my wet clothes and given me food and shelter. After that it seemed only courteous to help them with their—er—activities.'

'But what of your family? Surely they were anxious for you? Did you contact them, let them know that you were safe?'

'No, I am ashamed to say that I did not— not immediately. I was young, and reckless, and there were another four years to run until I could claim my inheritance. I was not prepared to sit back quietly and wait for time to pass.'

'Now *that* I do understand!' declared Stacey. 'I believe if one has a dream one should follow it. Aunt Jayne says young ladies should remain quietly at home until a suitable husband comes along, but I think that is quite nonsensical, and especially now, when Rupert has been summoned to London and is being urged to marry another! How can I sit back and do nothing?'

'Exactly so, brat. My uncle had been given charge of my property until I reached five-and-twenty, and I could not bear to watch him living at my expense. I plied the coast with my new friends for the next several months, then MacCauley had the idea of travelling across France.'

'France! But that was . . . we were at war!'

Vivyan grinned.

'That made it all the more exciting! MacCauley and I were of an age, both with a love of adventure. We lived on our wits, making a little money at cards, changing our identity to suit the company. We parted in Paris. MacCauley went on to Italy and I lived as best I could until the time came to return to England.'

Eustacia was about to ask Vivyan how he had lived during those years in France, when the coach ran over a particularly rough patch of road, jolting so badly that its occupants were thrown out of their seats and found themselves in a tangled heap on the floor of the coach as it lurched to a stop.

CHAPTER THREE

'Are you hurt?' Vivyan helped Miss Marchant back on to he seat, and as soon as he had ascertained that she was not injured he climbed out, bidding her to remain in the coach. After a few minutes Eustacia succumbed to curiosity and climbed out on to the road, where she found Mr Lagallan and the coachman inspecting the timbers beneath the box seat.

The coachman was shaking his head.

'One o' the futchels is gone, sir. Snapped.'

'Hell and damnation!' muttered Vivyan. 'Can we go on?'

'No, sir. T'wouldn't be safe—it supports the fore-carriage, you see, and the sway bar. The whole thing could tip over as easy as winking.'

Vivyan looked thoughtful, tapping the ground as he considered the situation.

'There will be a carriage-maker in Reading, sir,' suggested the coachman. 'He should be able to fix it in a couple of hours.'

'You had best take the coach there.' Mr Lagallan took out a purse and handed it to the coachman. 'That should be enough, and to spare. There is a sizeable village a mile or so down the road with a decent little inn. We will walk there now. If the carriage cannot be ready by first thing tomorrow, you must hire a vehicle to fetch us, do you understand?'

The coachman tugged at his forelock and the footman unstrapped Eustacia's portmanteau and his master's overnight bag and put them on the road before helping the coachman to turn the broken carriage back towards Reading.

Mr Lagallan picked up the two bags and set off down the road.

'Why do we not walk back to The Star and put up there?' asked Eustacia, skipping along beside him.

'I am too well known there, and I want to expose you as little as possible to the public gaze in your disguise.'

'You mean, if I was not with you, you would be able to spend the night in comfort!' she muttered, conscience-stricken. 'As it is we must take pot-luck at a little inn, where the food could be terrible and the sheets might not be aired! Vivyan, I am so sorry to put you to all this trouble.'

His frown lifted. 'I doubt it will be as bad as that! Besides, you wanted adventure, did you not?'

'Yes, but I do not want you to be uncomfortable.'

He laughed at that. 'My dear child, adventures are always uncomfortable—and frequently dangerous!'

'Oh. I expect this seems a little tame to you.'

'It is certainly inconvenient.' He saw she was looking downcast and added, 'The broken carriage is not your fault, Stacey, and I have frequently stayed in places far less comfortable than a village inn.'

'When you were in France?'

'Yes, although I also spent some weeks as a guest in a most luxurious château.'

Laughing at her eager questions, Mr Lagallan told Eustacia something of his travels, but despite his carefully worded descriptions, she was shrewd enough to guess that he had not always lived as a gentleman.

'And have you come home to settle down?'

'That was my intention. I have spent the

past year putting my estates in order.'

'And is that why you have offered for Miss Pensford?'

'Yes. I have to marry someone.' He glanced at her. 'You do not approve?'

'I think one should marry for love.'

'That is not always possible.'

'But surely *you* have no need of a fortune. Why should you not marry someone you like?'

'I cannot recall having said I do not *like* Miss Pensford.'

'Now I have offended you.'

'Not at all.'

'Yes, I have. You have become very polite, and—and distant, so I know you are offended! Pray forgive me.'

Vivyan felt his anger evaporating.

'Do you mean to say I have been discourteous to you until now? Abhorrent brat!'

She chuckled. 'That is much better! Look, we are approaching the village. You had best let me carry my own bag now, or people may think you far too kind and grow suspicious.'

*   *   *

They reached the inn, a small tavern at the roadside with the ambitious name of The Golden Cockerel. The landlord was able to furnish them with two bedrooms, and showed them into a small, sparsely furnished room

28

that he proudly described as a private parlour. The landlady came in presently with a tray and promised there would be hot water in their bedchambers in a twinkling. Miss Marchant looked about the room and said cheerfully, 'Well, this is very comfortable.'

'A damned nuisance,' muttered Vivyan, closely inspecting one less than perfect boot. 'Not only are my Hessians covered in mud, but I fear there may be a scratch on the leather.'

'Oh. Are you not enjoying yourself?'

'Not at all!'

'Well, I think that is very poor-spirited of you! Just think how fortunate we are. Your carriage stopped just outside Reading, within easy reach of repair, and it is a very fine day for a walk. Imagine how uncomfortable it would have been to trudge here in the rain! And we have come upon a most delightful inn, with a good fire and the most delicious cake!'

Vivyan had pulled off his boots and was closely inspecting the damage.

'It doesn't look too bad; I just hope Perkins will be able to polish it out.'

'Of course he will.' Eustacia came over to him and handed him a cup of coffee. 'Will you not try the cake, sir? It is very good.'

'You are determined to be cheerful, are you not, Stacey?' He grinned up at her and drew a smiling response.

'Of course! There is nothing here to make one unhappy!' Mr Lagallan knew an impulse to pull the girl down on to his lap, and sternly repressed it. Instead he pulled on his boots again and stood up.

'I will take my coffee in my room, I think. I need to wash—I would advise you to do the same, Stacey—and perhaps to rest until dinner.'

'Have I said something wrong?'

The harsh look disappeared and he smiled, flicking her cheek with one careless finger.

'Of course not, child, but it has been a long day, and I wish to take advantage of this lull in our activity!'

*   *   *

As he plunged his hands into the bowl of water so thoughtfully provided by his hostess, Vivyan cursed himself for being so inept. He had seen the hurt in Eustacia's face as he had left her, but surely she should understand how wrong it was for them to be alone! She was so naïve, so trusting; it would be far too easy for him to abuse that trust.

'She is no more than a babe!' he muttered. 'And the sooner I hand over responsibility for her, the better!' Slipping off his coat, he threw himself on the bed. 'Damnation—the girl is under my protection! Besides, she is in love with another man. And she is so innocent. If I give in to a desire to kiss her, that innocence would be lost for ever!'

Vivyan dozed fitfully, but after an hour he gave up all attempts to sleep and went downstairs to the parlour. Finding his young companion was not there, Vivyan made his way to Stacey's room. There was no reply to his knock and when he tried the handle, the door opened easily on to the empty room. Frowning, Mr Lagallan went outside into the yard, where the landlord was busy cutting logs.

'The young gentleman?' In answer to his question the landlord paused, resting his axe lightly upon one broad shoulder. 'Why, sir, he went off with our Davy to see a mill.'

'A mill?'

'Aye, sir. At Jenner's field. The young master being at a loose end, so to speak, and looking so down in the mouth, our Davy asks him if he wanted to go with 'un.' Something of Vivyan's dismay was apparent in his face, for the landlord continued, 'Lord love you, sir, you've no need to worry about the lad—he'll come to no 'arm, my boy'll see to that, and he'll bring the young master back safe afore dark, never fear.'

Stifling his misgivings, Mr Lagallan asked directions to the mill and, pausing only to fetch his cane, he set out for Jenner's field.

*　　　*　　　*

As Eustacia and her young escort trudged along the leafy lane, the innkeeper's son

31

whiled away the journey with tales of other mills he had seen. Most of these stories were apocryphal and couched in such cant terms that Miss Marchant understood only one word in twenty. Davy was a young man of about fifteen, very sturdily built and with an open, friendly nature. They had struck up a conversation within minutes of Stacey wandering into the inn-yard and, unwilling to appear churlish, Miss Marchant had accepted Davy's invitation, reasoning that it would at least while away the hours until dinner-time.

When they reached Jenner's field, the area was already thronging with spectators and Davy bemoaned the fact that all the best places in the nearby trees were taken. He moved away from the gate, where two men were busy collecting entrance fees, and pushed his way through a gap in the hedge before guiding Stacey to a steep embankment at the far side of the field.

'This be a capital vantage-point,' he remarked in his slow drawl. 'We shall see everything from 'ere.'

Looking down from her capital vantage-point, Eustacia realized with horror that she was about to witness a prize-fight. In the safety of the inn-yard, when her new acquaintance had spoken of a mill and talked of gentlemen, and form, and science, she had visualized some sort of educational talk or exhibition, and it was not until she saw the two men stripped to the waist, their faces already disfigured by years of brutal combat, that she understood the nature of the entertainment she was about to witness.

Young Davy drew a flask from his pocket, raised it to his lips and afterwards offered it to Stacey. She shook her head, her mind working quickly to think of an excuse to leave the scene without arousing any suspicion. The field was filling up now, and the noise of the crowd rose and fell on the cold, clear air. Davy pointed towards the clearing where the two opponents were limbering up.

'Look—my money'd be on Ted Barker, the man standing nearest that old beech tree. He's known as the Fox, 'cos he's a wily old devil. He ain't as big as Jameson, but he's quick, and unless Jameson can get in a well-aimed hit in the first few rounds, it's ames ace to a monkey the Fox'll win the day.'

Following his outstretched arm, Stacey observed the preparations taking place for the contest. Her eyes were drawn to a tall figure in a drab boxcoat, talking to the pugilist Davy had called Ted Barker. He looked vaguely familiar, and she realized it was Nathan MacCauley, the man she and Vivyan had met at The Star. She tried to shrink down between her companions, turning up the collar of her coat and praying that he was too far away to recognize her.

Listening to Davy's discourse, Stacey

33

nodded and tried to look interested. Across the field, she saw several smart carriages pulled up alongside the farm wagons, and she realized with some surprise that a large number of gentlemen were in attendance. She shivered. Even in the bright afternoon sun the spring air was cold, and her thin wool jacket was not as warm as the thick homespuns worn by most of the other spectators. The crowd was growing restless, waiting for the fight to begin, with catcalls and curses filling the air. Eustacia began to feel very uneasy.

'So there you are!'

The hand upon her shoulder made her jump, and she looked round guiltily.

'Vivyan!' At the sight of his stern face she almost cried with relief.

Pulling her to her feet, he said roughly, 'Come along, young man. I promised your mama I'd keep you out of mischief until you were safe at home again.'

Young Davy jumped up, looking anxious.

'Sir—there's nothin' amiss, is there? I didn't see no 'arm in bringin' the young master to a mill, honest I didn't.'

'No, the fault's not yours, I'm sure,' Mr Lagallan assured him. 'My young friend is far too ready for any spree, but *not* while under my care!'

There were several sympathetic murmurs from those nearby for Vivyan to let the lad be, and one or two mutters that he was blocking

34

the view. Mr Lagallan threw Davy an apologetic glance, then turned back to Miss Marchant.

'An oath is an oath, Stacey. Your friend can stay and enjoy the mill, but you had best come with me.' He gripped her elbow and guided her through the crowd and out of the field.

*   *   *

When they reached the lane, Eustacia gave a huge sigh. 'I was *so* glad to see you! Vivyan, it is a *prizefight!*'

'Well, what were you expecting?'

'I don't know—a fair, perhaps, or some sort of lecture.' She looked offended when he threw back his head and laughed. 'Well, how was I to know what it would be?'

They began to walk back towards the inn.

'You were not to know at all, my innocent. I hope you have learned your lesson and will not go off with strangers again.'

'Oh I have, Vivyan, truly! But when you went off to your room, I did not know what to do, and I went out into the yard, and Davy and I started talking, and—and here I am.' She took his arm, and leaned against him. 'I was never so relieved to see anyone in my life! How did you find me?'

'Easily. That carrot-top of yours proved very useful on this occasion.'

'My wretched hair! How I wish it were dark,

35

or even better—fashionably fair.'

Vivyan stopped. 'That is the first missish thing I have heard you say, and let me tell you, it don't become you. You have beautiful hair. It's my favourite colour.'

Eustacia blushed. 'Truly, Vivyan? Y-you like it?'

'Truly.' He grinned, touching her nose with the tip of one finger. 'And I think freckles are very . . . enchanting.'

For a moment she gazed up at him, her eyes shining, then with a sigh she shook her head and turned to walk on.

'No,' she said sadly. 'It is very kind of you to say so, Vivyan, but I know that red hair is not at all fashionable—and that makes it all the more wonderful that Rupert should love me, don't you think?'

'No,' murmured Vivyan, looking at the slim figure striding ahead of him. 'No, it is not wonderful at all.'

*　　　*　　　*

After a substantial dinner, Eustacia suggested they should take a stroll in the lane. She quickly brushed aside Mr Lagallan's objections.

'I am not at all sleepy, Vivyan, and there is nothing to do here. No games or books—and there is nothing worse than tossing and turning all night because one is not tired!'

36

Mr Lagallan tried one last objection.

'You have no coat, brat.'

'But the wind has dropped, and I promise you I will not feel the cold, as long as we keep moving.'

So Mr Lagallan stifled his conscience and accompanied Miss Marchant outside. The rising moon was just high enough to light their way, and Vivyan pointed out to his companion the stars and planets that were still visible in the clear sky. Eustacia, her hand tucked into his arm, sighed.

'How I wish I had learned astronomy! Miss Frobisher was very good, but she was concerned that we should learn to draw, and paint, and play the pianoforte.'

'But they are very necessary accomplishments, child.'

'Perhaps, but if I had learned astronomy, I would be able to navigate my way around the world!' She laughed and glanced up at him. 'You think that very fanciful, I suppose, but apart from my one season in London, I have never been away from home before, and I would so love to travel. That is why I am enjoying this adventure so much. But I expect it seems very tame to you, for you have been adventuring all over Europe, and I have no doubt you found yourself in situations far more perilous than a quiet country lane!'

'Yet I can assure you, nymph, that I have rarely enjoyed myself more.'

Miss Marchant did not reply to this. She merely squeezed his arm and walked on beside him.

Presently she spoke again. 'I noticed any number of very modish carriages at Jenner's field today. Do gentlemen enjoy watching such things, Vivyan?'

'In the main, I think they do.'

'Do you?'

'Sometimes, but I much prefer to take part.'

She stared at him. 'You like to *fight*? What if you should be hurt?'

'Ah, the skill is to avoid such a thing.' He smiled down at her. 'I practise regularly at Jackson's parlour in London.'

She frowned. 'Well, I think it is a horrid thing to do. Why should you wish to hurt a fellow human being?'

'I think I must be sadly decadent,' he responded meekly.

They were approaching a crossroads, the trees on each side of the road threw out thick black branches across the highway, plunging the road into deepest shadow. Vivyan was about to suggest they should turn back, when they heard voices ahead. They stopped and Vivyan put his hand on Stacey's lips to silence her inevitable question. The voices grew louder, as if in argument. Vivyan drew Eustacia deeper into the shadows as the voices were replaced by a series of sharp thuds and grunts. Eustacia tried to move, but Vivyan held

38

her fast.

'Not yet!' he hissed.

The scuffling continued, then there was a sharp cry. Unable to bear the inactivity, Eustacia wrenched herself free and set off towards the sounds of the mêlée.

'This way, lads!' she called, her voice as loud and gruff as she could make it. 'John, bring up the dogs—Reuben, hand me my pistol!'

With an oath Vivyan followed, catching up with Stacey just as she reached the crossroads, where she stopped. The trees and bushes had been cut back from the road at this point, and in the pale gleam of the moonlight they saw a black shape crumpled on the ground, while two figures were running away, disappearing into the darkness.

'It's all right,' gasped Eustacia, breathing heavily, 'they've gone.' She hurried towards the figure on the ground, Vivyan beside her, muttering furiously.

'You damned little fool! You do not know what you might have found around this corner!'

'Admit it, Vivyan, if I had not been here, you would not have held back.'

'Perhaps, but—'

Stacey was not listening. They had reached the body and Eustacia fell to her knees, searching for signs of life.

'He breathes!' she exclaimed, and gasped as Vivyan turned the man over to expose his face to the moonlight.

'It's the man we saw in Reading!' Eustacia stared down at the unconscious figure. Blood had darkened his long fair hair, and trickled from his mouth and nose. There was a cut on his cheek, and a livid bruise was already forming around one eye.

'We can't leave him here, Vivyan. We must get him to the inn.' She rose unsteadily to her feet.

'I'll carry him,' said Mr Lagallan. 'Here, you take his hat and cane.'

'I could run back and fetch help—'

'No! I'm not letting you out of my sight if there are footpads on the prowl. Stay with me.'

Obediently, Stacey picked up the hat and cane, and walked silently beside Vivyan, who had hoisted the unconscious figure over his shoulder and was striding back to The Golden Cockerel. As they reached the inn, she ran before him, shouting for the landlord. That worthy came bustling out, his eyes widening as Mr Lagallan staggered in.

'Quick, man! Help me get him upstairs to a bed. Footpads.'

'B-but we've no more rooms free, sir!'

'Then put him in mine.' Gently, Vivyan lowered MacCauley into the arms of the landlord and his tapster. Miss Marchant was about to follow the little group up the stairs when Vivyan gave her a curt command to wait for him in the parlour. Alone in the little

40

room, she threw more logs on to the fire and sat down at the table, suddenly feeling very weak. She chided herself for her sudden desire to cry: she had wanted adventure, and she must not disappoint Vivyan! Thus when Mr Lagallan came down stairs some time later, he found Miss Marchant finishing a cup of hot milk. She was very pale, but composed.

'I ordered you some brandy, sir.' She managed a small smile. 'I did not think you would want milk.'

'True, brat. Thank you.'

'How is Mr MacCauley?'

'Unconscious. He has been badly beaten, but there are no bones broken, save perhaps a couple of ribs. The landlord will send for the doctor in the morning, and I'll leave enough money to pay his shot.'

'You will not leave him here!'

'I must get you to London, Stacey.'

She looked as if she would argue, but the entrance of the landlord made her bite her tongue.

'Beggin' your pardon, sir. The gentleman's as comfortable as we can make 'im now, sir. I'll send my lad for the doctor first thing. And I've set up a truckle-bed for you in the little room at the end of the passage, sir, though the young master's bed is big enough for two . . .'

'No, no, my cousin is such a dashed fidget I'd get no sleep at all! The small room will do very well for me, thank you.'

41

As the landlord withdrew, Eustacia gave a little smile.

'A truckle-bed! Poor Vivyan.'

He laughed and finished the rest of the brandy.

'I've slept on worse!' He stood up. 'Now, brat, get yourself off to bed. We make an early start in the morning.'

CHAPTER FOUR

Eustacia tossed and turned in the hard bed, listening to the noises outside her door. Footsteps padded up and down the passage, and once she heard the landlord berating one of his minions in the hallway below. However, The Golden Cockerel was not a coaching-inn, nor was it on a main road, and as the night wore on the inn fell silent, with only the creaking of the timbers or a mouse gnawing at the wainscot to disturb the peace. Still Eustacia could not sleep: she did not know whether it was because of the strange surroundings or the excitement of the evening, but she was wide awake. The moon, climbing in a cloudless sky, shone in through the little casement window and she lay still in the semi-darkness, allowing her mind to drift over the events of the day. After a while her attention was caught by a noise coming from the next room. Through the thin partition she heard a violent coughing, then a long, drawn-out groan. She knew it must be the man MacCauley and she listened, hoping that Vivyan or the landlord would attend him, but there was only silence, then a few moments later she heard another groan.

It was not in Miss Marchant's nature to ignore any creature in distress, and although her heart was thudding so heavily she could hardly breathe, she slipped out of bed, pulled on her boy's shirt and breeches and tiptoed to the door. An oil-lamp burned on the landing and in its pale light she could see the length of the passage. All the doors were shut and she hesitated, wondering which one was Vivyan's. She heard another cough and a stifled curse from MacCauley's room and, with sudden decision, she opened the door and peered cautiously in. The room was lit only by the moon, but it was sufficient for Stacey to see the figure on the bed. MacCauley turned his head and peered towards the door.

'Who's there?'

'It's—it's me, sir. Mr Lagallan and I found you and brought you here, to the inn.'

There was a pause. Stacey wondered if MacCauley remembered her.

'Ah yes, by heaven. Saw you at The Star, did I not? Fore Gad I hurt! Fetch me a light, boy.'

Straining her eyes against the darkness, Stacey found the tinderbox and managed to light the candle in its holder beside the bed. Signs of the night's activity still remained: MacCauley's clothes had been hastily removed and thrown over a chair beside the bed, and a grey cloth floated in the wash-bowl on a side table, next to a pile of ragged bandages that had been prepared but not used. Stacey hesitated, staring down at the bruised and beaten face of Nathan MacCauley.

Lying back against the pillows, his straight, fair hair falling over his brow, he looked gaunt and tired, and for a few moments he lay still, his eyes closed and his breathing shallow and laboured. Stacey was about to move away when he spoke again.

'What time is it?' Observing Stacey's hesitation, MacCauley waved one hand towards his clothes. 'You will find a pocket-watch in my waistcoat—if it wasn't filched or smashed to pieces in the beating.'

Eustacia searched through the dark tangle of clothes until her fingers found the watch. She brought it over to the light.

'No, it's not broken. It wants but twenty minutes to midnight.'

'Then I am not too late!' MacCauley threw back the bedclothes.

'What are you doing?' Stacey averted her eyes from the sight of his bruised body, thankful that when Vivyan had undressed MacCauley he had left him wearing his under-drawers.

44

'I am getting up.'

'No, no, you are not well!' She put her hands on his shoulders and gently pushed him back into bed. 'Pray lie down again, sir.'

MacCauley gave up the struggle, one hand pressed to his ribs as his face registered the pain. Stacey watched him anxiously.

'I *shall* do this!' he muttered. He turned his fierce stare upon Stacey. 'Help me into my clothes!'

'No, sir, I cannot do that.'

'Damn your eyes, do as you are told!'

'I will not!' hissed Stacey. 'And if you persist, I will call my c-cousin Vivyan to help subdue you!'

MacCauley fell back, a speculative look in his eye.

'Oh-ho! Cousin Vivyan, is it? Well, we'll see.' He rolled towards the edge of the bed and swung his legs to the floor.

Eustacia, her eyes wide with alarm, was about to run to the door when she saw a spasm of pain cross MacCauley's face. With a groan, he fell back against the pillows. Gently, she lifted his legs back on to the bed.

'Now, sir, will you believe that you cannot get up?' She spoke gruffly, pulling the covers delicately over his bruised body.

He did not reply, but his laboured breathing told her he was in pain. She picked up the damp cloth and wiped his face, relieved to see the furrowed creases in his brow disappearing.

'Oh, pray you, sir, do not attempt to get up again.'

'But I must! I have to see—' He sighed, as if admitting his weakness. He turned his eyes towards Stacey.

'If I cannot go—will you go for me?'

'M-me . . . ? G-go where?'

'I have to meet . . . a man. At the crossroads, where you found me. I am to meet him at midnight. If you are quick, he will still be there!'

'But—but I can't, I won't—'

'Then, by God, you must let me get up!'

'No, no—wait! Why is it so important to see this man?'

'He—has papers—information about . . .' He hesitated, glancing speculatively at her. 'About me. As I told Lagallan, I've a mind to turn respectable, as he has done, but these papers could land me in Newgate.' Again that hard stare was bent on Stacey. 'Will you go?'

'But—how? I mean, if this man is a villain . . .'

'Nay, Gibson's a petty rogue, but he's a man of his word. You'll be safe enough, if that's your worry.' He drew the ring from his little finger. 'Here, give him this and my pocket-watch—I was to give him a purse, but Barker's friends took all I had, so he must make do with these. In any event, they'll fetch more than I agreed to pay him. Go, lad—hurry now!'

Stacey hesitated.

'How—how will I know this man?'

46

MacCauley laughed, ending in a gasp as the effort tore at his bruised ribs.

'How many people d'ye expect to see abroad on a lonely road at midnight? Begone, boy!' Stacey moved to the door. 'Wait! How old are you?'

'I'm . . . I am fifteen, sir.'

'Hmm, not a lot to you, is there? You'd better take my cane with you—now hurry!'

*   *   *

When Stacey had strolled along the lane earlier that evening with Vivyan, she had been entranced by the starry night. Now, even with the moon riding high overhead in the clear sky, the world seemed a much more frightening place. The trees cast dark shadows across the road, and the silence, which had seemed so peaceful with Vivyan at her side, now seemed fraught with menace. Telling herself there was nothing to fear, she clutched MacCauley's cane and walked quickly along the lane towards the crossroads. The road seemed much longer than she remembered, and the sudden screech of a vixen made her jump half-way across the lane. She forced herself to walk on, her heart pounding painfully against her ribs. At last the crossroads was in sight, and she saw a shadowed figure walking up and down. Calmer now that she could see her quarry, Stacey moved forward.

'Are—are you come to meet M-Mr MacCauley?'

The figure turned towards her. He was a small man, his sharp features accentuated by the moonlight.

'And what if I am?'

'He is in-indisposed, and has sent me in his stead.' Eustacia tried to make her voice as deep and gruff as possible, but to her own ears the words came out in a squeak. 'Do you have the papers? Show me.'

The man reached into his coat and pulled out a packet. 'They are all here. Do you have the money?'

'No—but I have something much more valuable!' she added quickly, as the man swore and started to return the papers to his pocket. 'Look!' She drew out the watch and ring. 'These are worth far more than the agreed sum.'

The man drew back. 'I told 'im I wanted coin! I ain't no fencing cove!'

Stacey shrugged.

'The ring alone is worth a year's wages,' she said, carelessly. 'It's solid gold. But if it must be cash, we cannot trade . . .' She turned away, holding her breath.

'No—wait!'

Stacey uttered up a silent prayer.

'Solid gold, you say?' The man licked his lips. 'And I can take the watch as well?'

48

'Yes.'

'Very well. Give 'em to me.'

'Let me have the letters first.'

Cautiously, they approached each other and the exchange was made. The man seemed to relax and his teeth gleamed in the moonlight.

'Tell MacCauley I'm obliged to 'im.' Touching his hat, he strode off, whistling, and Stacey, after a final look at the retreating figure, took to her heels and fled back to the inn.

*   *   *

Eustacia crept up the stairs and paused at the door to MacCauley's room, trying to recover her breath after her headlong flight. After a few moments, she opened the door and went in. The candle still burned beside the bed, and MacCauley looked towards her.

'Well, did you get the letters?'

'Yes, they are here.'

He snatched the packet from her hands, quickly scanning the closely written pages. He threw a quick glance at Stacey.

'Did you read these?'

'Of course not!'

'No, you would not do that, would you? Here, then. Put them in my coat and you may go back to bed, I have no more need of you.' He watched her, a slight grimace creasing his brow, and as she made for the door, he called

49

her back.

'Yes, sir? Are you in pain? Shall I pour you a little water?'

'Aye.'

Stacey half-filled a cup and held it to MacCauley's parched lips. As he lay back against the pillows, she was aware that his gaze had become more intent. He grasped her wrist.

'What do they call you?'

Stacey quickly searched her memory—had Vivyan given her name to MacCauley? She thought not.

'Stacey, sir. S-Stacey Charlton.'

'Lagallan's cousin, you say? I disremember Lagallan mentioning a cousin when we was in France.'

'And why should you?' said a cool voice from the doorway. 'I don't rattle on about every brat in my family.' Vivyan came into the room. Stacey noticed that he was still dressed, although he had discarded his coat and his waistcoat was undone. He frowned at her. 'How long have you been here?'

She felt the fingers on her wrist tighten.

'Not—not long, Si—cousin.'

Vivyan glanced towards the bed. 'So, you are awake.' MacCauley released Eustacia and shifted in the bed, wincing slightly.

'Aye. Did you bring me here? Mighty obliged to you.'

A slight smile dispelled Vivyan's frown.

'It would not be civilized to leave you cluttering the highway. Who attacked you?'

MacCauley's gaze shifted away.

'Didn't see 'em. Footpads, most likely.'

'Do you think me a fool, Nathan? Who were you trying to trick this time?'

MacCauley grinned, gasping as the movement tore at his bruised muscles.

'I was Barker's umpire at the mill this afternoon, and was involved in arranging some of the bets. Unfortunately, my—er—expenses were greater than anticipated. Barker lost, and his family were none too pleased, thought I'd let their man down.'

MacCauley shivered, and Miss Marchant pulled the blankets up over his bruised chest. Vivyan's black brows drew together.

'Stacey—go to bed.'

Biting her lip against a sharp retort, she obeyed the curt command in silence, closing the door quietly behind her.

'Did you pay Barker to throw the fight?' Vivyan enquired.

'What sort of rum cove d'you think I am?' demanded MacCauley, offended. 'I promised Barker a cut of the takings, and told him I'd settle up once I'd been to Town. Word of a gentleman.'

Mr Lagallan's teeth gleamed.

'Coming it too thick, Nathan.'

'No, 'tis the truth! I was *born* a gentleman, after all, and once I've signed the papers and

51

have secured my inheritance, I intend to live like one. That little affair with Barker was my last deal. I'm a free man now. At least I would be, only . . .'

'Only?'

Wry amusement gleamed in the grey eyes. 'They took my purse, Viv.'

Mr Lagallan grinned.

'I'll pay your shot here, plus enough for the doctor who is coming to see you tomorrow, *and* I'll give you your fare to London.'

'You are monstrous generous, Viv. You have my word that I'll settle with you once I get to Town—'

'No!' Mr Lagallan stopped him. 'I'd prefer to have your word that you will keep out of my way once you get there!'

CHAPTER FIVE

The repaired coach duly arrived at The Golden Cockerel the following morning to collect Mr Lagallan and his companion. Miss Marchant looked a trifle heavy-eyed, but she was eager to talk over the events of the evening. Mr Lagallan refused to discuss anything until they were on their way. Eustacia scarcely waited for the steps to be put up before she bombarded her companion with questions.

'How is Mr MacCauley this morning? What did he say to you—did he tell you who had attacked him?'

Mr Lagallan threw up his hands, laughing at her.

'Gently, my child. Give me time to answer one question before you fire another!'

'But the poor man was so bruised and battered, I thought perhaps we should have stayed to nurse him.'

'Now I *know* your wits have gone begging! I wouldn't wager a groat against MacCauley seeing through your disguise if he saw you for any length of time.'

Eustacia wondered what Mr Lagallan would say if he knew of her midnight dealings with the injured man. She was considering telling him the whole tale, when he spoke again.

'And why the deuce did you go into his room last night? Of all the ill-considered starts! You should have called me!'

'He was moaning so pitifully.'

'And you wanted to be a ministering angel! Hare-brained little ninny!'

Miss Marchant held her tongue, and Mr Lagallan's harsh look faded as she fought back an angry retort.

'You do well not to come to blows with me, brat! I'll give you credit for a kind heart, my dear, but don't waste your sympathy on Nathan MacCauley. The doctor will attend him today and I've paid the landlord well for his trouble, so you may put the matter out of your mind.'

Impulsively, she caught his hand.

'You are such a kind person, Vivyan, and you have been so good to me, I do not know how I shall ever repay you.'

He laughed, squeezing her fingers.

'Nay, child, I shall consider it reward enough if we can get you to your godmama without a scandal!'

*   *   *

The remainder of the journey was accomplished with no further mishap and in good time, so that it was early afternoon when the pair were shown into the morning-room of Major Lagallan's house in Bruton Street by a wooden-faced footman.

'Cheer up, no one's going to eat you.' Vivyan nodded encouragingly at Eustacia, but although that young lady forced a smile the shadow of anxiety remained in her eyes. She was wrapped in Vivyan's large travelling-cloak, and at the sounds of someone approaching, she clutched it even tighter about her and moved a little closer to Vivyan.

Mrs Lagallan came into the room, her ready smile upon her lips as she greeted her brother-in-law.

'Viv, my dear! Philip will be so sorry he is not here to meet you!' Her glance flickered over Miss Marchant, and she looked back at Vivyan, her brows drawing together slightly. 'Will you not introduce me to your companion?'

Vivyan gave his sister-in-law his most charming grin which immediately set her on her guard.

'Caro, I need your help. This is Miss Eustacia Marchant.' Eustacia flushed under the scrutiny of Mrs Lagallan's steady grey eyes and she heard the laughter in Vivyan's voice as he continued, 'It was expedient for Miss Marchant to travel here—ah—in disguise.'

The silence stretched for a full minute before Mrs Lagallan spoke. Without taking her eyes from Eustacia, she said carefully, 'I think you had best explain, Vivyan.'

Mr Lagallan guided Miss Marchant to a chair and obliged her to sit down. The cloak fell open, and Vivyan bit back a smile as he observed Mrs Lagallan's look of surprise as her guest's breeches and stockings were thus exposed.

'Darling Caro!' He pushed his sister-in-law gently on to the sofa, and sat down beside her. 'I knew you would not disappoint me! Any other woman would have fallen into hysterics at this point.'

'And I may well do so if you do not explain immediately!'

'Very well! I was returning from Combe Charlton, having proposed to Miss Pensford,

55

when Stacey—Miss Marchant—fell into my arms.'

Frowning at Vivyan's levity, Eustacia judged it time to speak.

'You see, ma'am, I was stuck, in a tree. Viv—Mr Lagallan—rescued me and—and then, because I would not let him take me home, he offered to escort me to London, which was excessively kind of him.'

'Y—yes, wasn't it?' murmured Caroline.

'Stacey has come to Town to find a certain gentleman. She thought it safest to travel as a boy, but I immediately saw through her disguise, and thought that if I could discover her secret so easily, on no account should she wander the country unprotected.'

'No, of course not.'

Observing that his sister-in-law was far from happy, he said quietly, 'Miss Marchant has a little baggage with her, Caro. Perhaps it would be best if she changed into her gown before we continue this discussion, for I feel sure it would be more comfortable—for all of us.'

Recalled to her duty, Caroline rose.

'Of course, how thoughtless of me.' She glanced at Eustacia and, observing the young lady's anxious countenance, smiled at her, saying gently: 'Come, my dear. I will show you to one of the guest rooms and my maid shall help you to change. You must not worry, for she is the very soul of discretion . . .' The two ladies left the room, but Caroline reappeared

56

a few minutes later, and advanced upon Vivyan.

'Now, sir, let me have the truth, if you please!'

'No need to look so fierce, Caro! I vow I positively quake at the sight of you.'

'Don't try to turn me up sweet, Viv. I am inured to your charms.'

He led her back to the sofa.

'Very well, Caroline. Sit down, and you shall have the word with no bark on it.'

Mrs Lagallan listened in silence while Vivyan described his meeting with Eustacia, and their journey to London. When he had finished, he reached for her hands, saying coaxingly, 'I need your help on this, Caro. If you will not support us, the child's reputation is ruined.'

'With no thanks to you! In heaven's name, why did you not take the child back to her grandfather?'

'She would have objected most strongly to that, and in any event I have no doubt she would have run off again as soon as I was out of sight. No, my dear. Stacey was determined to get to London. But you have talked to her, you must see that she is such an innocent she could not be allowed to travel alone?'

'Are you *sure* she is such a babe, Vivyan? Perhaps she is set on entrapping you.'

Mr Lagallan smiled, a rueful look in his eyes.

'Lord, Caro, when you have been in her company a little longer you will know that she is head over heels in love with this Mr Alleyne of hers. She has no thought of me, other than as a friend.'

'A novel experience for you,' she said, an answering gleam in her own grey eyes. 'Well, we had best do what we can to unravel this coil. The girl must be handed over to her godmother, and if we can do that without a breath of scandal, we are home free. You are sure no one saw Miss Marchant in your company?'

Vivyan thought of the meeting on the road with Nathan MacCauley.

'No one of consequence.'

'Good. Then I think it will be best if we tell Lady Bilderston that it was I who came upon Miss Marchant and took her up with me.'

'Well done, Caro, my love! I knew I could rely on you!'

She coloured faintly: even after so many years, she was not so impervious to his charms as she professed.

'You had best go away now, Vivyan. We will expect you here for dinner, and in the meantime I must think how I am going to explain all this to Philip. I fear he will think I am run mad!'

But when Vivyan was shown into the drawing-room in Bruton Street some hours later, he found his brother and sister-in-law in apparent domestic harmony. Major Lagallan greeted his brother with his habitual good humour unimpaired.

'Well, little brother, you have a novel way of settling down.'

Vivyan grinned. 'Caroline has told you everything?'

'Yes. And I have talked with Miss Marchant. She is clearly a gently bred young lady, albeit very determined to have her way.'

'Aye, full of spirit! But such a babe, Philip. I could not leave her at Bath.'

'No, indeed. But this young man she talks of, do you know him?'

'Rupert Alleyne? No. I fear he is some young buck who whiled away a few idle weeks flirting with a pretty girl. The devil of it is she's taken it to heart! But she is determined to find him, and confident that he loves her.'

'You do not think that is so?' put in Caroline.

'I fear she is going to be disappointed.' Vivyan broke off as the door opened, and he turned to see Miss Marchant enter.

Gone were the brown wool suit and the badly tied neckcloth, replaced with a fine muslin gown embroidered with dainty yellow flowers. Miss Marchant's hair, freed from the confining ribbon, had been coaxed into shining red-gold curls about her head.

Mr Lagallan bowed.

'My compliments, Caro. You have turned

my wood nymph into a princess.'

Observing Eustacia's blush, Caroline took her arm and gave her an encouraging smile.

'I deserve no credit, Vivyan. I merely sent my maid to help Eustacia to dress.'

But this Miss Marchant would not allow.

'Indeed, ma'am, you have been more than kind to me!' she said. 'You furnished me with soap, and a hot bath, and have treated me with such kindness, I cannot thank you enough.'

'Nonsense, child. We are delighted to help you. Now, come and sit beside me, my dear, and we will tell Vivyan what we have decided.'

Major Lagallan cast a rueful glance at his brother.

'It would appear that we are now mere auditors in this matter, Viv.'

Caroline frowned at him.

'Be serious, Philip. Vivyan; Eustacia and I discussed the matter most thoroughly after you had left us. She has given me Lady Bilderston's direction, and I have already sent a note to that lady, and received a reply that I may call upon her in the morning.'

'And does she know the reason for your visit?' asked Vivyan.

'No. I shall take Eustacia with me, and we will throw ourselves on her mercy.'

'If you tell her everything, she'll probably be carried off with apoplexy,' murmured Vivyan, grinning.

Eustacia giggled. 'No, of course it would not

do to tell her *everything!* We will say that it was Caroline who took me up when she learned I was determined to come to London. And Caroline thinks it would be best not to tell Godmama that I came here to find Rupert. Also,' she fixed her anxious gaze upon Mr Lagallan, 'I hope you are not offended, Vivyan, but Caroline thought it best if we say you and I had not met until now.'

Vivyan's eyes danced.

'Not at all. And do you think Lady Bilderston will take you in?'

'Well, I hope so,' said Stacey, wrinkling her brow, 'but if she does not, it does not matter, for Caroline has said I may stay here while we write to my grandfather, and *that* will give me time to find Rupert!'

*　　*　　*

Miss Marchant's sunny spirits were slightly more subduded the next morning as she accompanied Mrs Lagallan to Fanshawe Gardens. An elderly butler escorted them to the blue saloon and announced them in funereal terms. Entering a few paces behind Caroline, Eustacia nervously studied Lady Bilderston. She was insensibly cheered by the picture her godmother presented. Lady Bilderston had risen to greet them, and it was seen that she was of average height, but much more than average girth. However her countenance was kindly, and she immediately came forward, saying with a smile, 'My dear Mrs Lagallan! I was in a quandary to know just why you should wish to see me, but as soon as Avebury announced you, I realized! You have brought my god-daughter to see me! How delightful!' She turned towards Miss Marchant, holding out her hands. 'So you are little Eustacia! Goodness, how you have grown; I think I cannot have seen you since you were an infant! Well, well, you are a pretty little thing, and no mistake! You have very much your mother's looks, although her hair was a little less red than yours, I think. Come and give me a kiss, there's a good girl.'

Somewhat dazed, Eustacia saluted the powdered cheek presented to her. Lady Bilderston invited them to sit down, ordered Avebury to bring refreshments, and sank once again on to the sofa.

'How kind of you to visit me. Are you making a long stay in Town, my dear?'

'To be quite open with you, Lady Bilderston, that depends upon yourself,' replied Mrs Lagallan. Favouring the advantage of attack, she waited only for the door to close upon the butler before launching into the explanation of Eustacia's presence in London. Lady Bilderston looked a little bewildered at first, and at the end of the tale she frowned at Miss Marchant.

It was extremely ill-advised to set out alone,

my dear,' she said, gently.

Emboldened by this temperate response, Eustacia said earnestly: 'Oh, I know it was very wrong of me, Godmama, but I was so *desperate* to come here, and I could think of no other way! Pray do not be angry with me.'

'The thing is, ma'am, what is to be done now?' said Caroline.

Lady Bilderston looked nonplussed, and was relieved that the entrance of Avebury with a tray of refreshments prevented her answering immediately.

She had been a widow for some twenty years, and lived a very comfortable life in Town, making occasional visits to her friends and indulging in a very indolent lifestyle. The eruption into her settled world of an energetic young lady was not at all what she had envisaged, and would most certainly upset her comfortable regime. However, she had a kindly disposition, and found she was not proof against the look of hopeful anticipation on her god-daughter's countenance.

'Well, Eustacia must come to me, of course. Poor child. I can see that to be cooped up in the country when you are longing for balls and parties must be very frustrating. We will write to Sir Jasper immediately, and if he is agreeable, you shall stay with me for a long visit. Only,' Lady Bilderston looked a little anxious, 'you must understand, Eustacia, that I rarely entertain, nor do I go into society a great deal.'

Eustacia looked a little disappointed, but she rallied, saying, 'Oh—oh, well, it is so very dull in Somerset that I am sure I shall find even the smallest party exciting.'

'And if you would not object, ma'am, I should be delighted to take Eustacia about with me occasionally,' put in Caroline, winning a grateful look from Miss Marchant.

'Well, that is not to say we won't take in a few select assemblies,' said Lady Bilderston, mentally reviewing her acquaintances, 'and then there is Snuffles, my little dog. I am sure you would enjoy walking him for me.'

Eustacia gave her a dazzling smile. 'That would be delightful, Godmama.'

*   *   *

'Well—Stacey is not with you, so I presume Lady Bilderston has taken her in?'

Mrs Lagallan sank on to a sofa and eyed her brother-in-law with disfavour.

'I shall never know why I allow myself to be embroiled in your scrapes, Vivyan!'

'Because you can't resist my charm! So, the old lady has accepted her, and there's no scandal?'

'Yes, Lady Bilderston has agreed that Eustacia can stay with her, at least until they have a reply from Sir Jasper. I was in a quake lest she questioned me too closely, but she has

64

a most amiable disposition. I felt truly dreadful to be imposing on her, for she has not seen the child for years, and I was afraid at first that she would not own her. Of course, she thinks Eustacia is very forward, to have run away to London all on her own, but goodness knows what she would have made of the *true* story!'

Vivyan dropped down beside her and took her hand.

'Poor Caro, did you have to work very hard to persuade her? Never mind. Your part in the matter is over now, so you may be easy.'

'No, I may not!' retorted Mrs Lagallan. 'I have told Lady Bilderston that I will take the child out with me now and again, for I could see that the poor woman was wondering just how she was to entertain a lively young girl every day of the week! Besides,' she admitted, 'I like Eustacia, and I am very much afraid that when she finds this Rupert Alleyne, she is going to be dreadfully hurt.'

The smile left Vivyan's eyes.

'I think so, too. But I'm hoping that the novelty of going into society might help her forget her infatuation. I'm glad you have befriended her, Caro, you may need to prevent her from embarking upon some other madcap scheme.'

*　　　*　　　*

Mrs Lagallan made her second visit to

Fanshawe Gardens a week later, when she invited Eustacia to drive in the park with her and take advantage of the mild spring weather. Miss Marchant was in excellent spirits, and lost no time in describing the whirl of activity that had engulfed her since their last meeting, ticking off on her fingers the dressmakers, milliners and seamstresses she had seen in the past seven days.

'Goodness!' exclaimed Caroline, laughter bubbling in her voice. 'Poor Lady Bilderston will be worn out by so much unaccustomed exertion!'

'No, no, for Godmama handed me over to Cardwell, her dresser, and it is she who has taken over all the arrangements. I admit I was terrified of her at first, for she can be a little sharp, but once she realized that Godmama wanted her to have the dressing of me, and that she was to spare no expense, she became quite excited about the matter. We have been to *dozens* of warehouses, and she has harried Godmama's poor seamstress into making up a few gowns for me immediately, because although we have had a reply from Grandpapa, and he has said I may stay, my trunks have not yet arrived.'

'Well, if the walking-dress you are wearing is one of her choices, then I think Lady Bilderston's dresser has excellent taste,' agreed Caroline. 'That shade of green is perfect for your colouring.'

Eustacia blushed, and thanked her for the compliment, but there was a slight crease between her brows as she added, 'I don't know when I am to wear all these new gowns, for Godmama tells me that she lives very quietly, and that I am not to expect to be going to parties every night. But if I do *not* go into society, how am I ever going to find Rupert?'

'I am sure Lady Bilderston does not mean to keep you as a recluse, my dear.'

'No, of course, but if we are to go to only a few very select parties, I may never meet Rupert!'

'Calm yourself, child. I have no doubt that if he is in Town, you will see him sooner or later, if not at a party then here in the park, or at the theatre.'

Eustacia looked doubtful. 'Yes, but I feel so helpless, just waiting to run into him! I thought perhaps I might ask Vivyan to make enquiries at the clubs, for he is very likely to be known in one of them, don't you think? Caroline, would you be kind enough to ask Vivyan if he would do so?'

Caroline smiled and patted Stacey's hands.

'Better still—you shall ask him yourself, for here he is coming towards us, and Philip is with him.' She directed Miss Marchant's gaze to the riders approaching, and Eustacia could not suppress a little thrill of pleasure when they turned their horses to walk on either side of the open carriage. She thought she had

never seen two finer horsemen: Major
Lagallan with his tall, upright figure was
mounted on a beautiful long-tailed grey, the
perfect foil for Vivyan and his rangy black
hunter. Vivyan tipped his hat to Stacey, and
smiled down at her.

'How is Lady Bilderston treating you, wood
nymph?'

'She is all kindness, and Grandpapa has
agreed to my staying in Town for the summer!'

'Excellent! I can see by your looks that you
are enjoying yourself in London.'

She cast a sparkling look at him.

'Oh, I am! It is very strange, but—when I
look out at the stars at night, I feel so happy,
just to know that Rupert is in the same town,
looking up at the same sky. Is that not
wonderful?'

'It makes me feel a trifle queasy!'

She laughed. 'That is because you have no
romance about you!' She cast a quick glance at
Mrs Lagallan, who was deep in conversation
with her husband. 'But, Vivyan, I do not know
how I am going to find Rupert. Can you go to
the clubs, and find out if he is known there?'

'I could, but I don't see how that will help
you.'

'Could you not arrange a meeting for us?'
Glancing up at him, she saw that his
expression was unusually grim. 'N-nothing
improper, of course,' she added hastily. 'B-but
if you could just see him, talk to him—

please, Vivyan.'

His frown melted as he met the anxious entreaty in her green eyes. He sighed.

'Very well. If you have no news of him within the next two weeks, I will see what I can do to find him, but I think we must then find some way for the two of you to meet as if by chance. After all, you don't want him to think you have followed him all the way to Town, do you?'

The little chin went up.

'Why not? It is the truth, after all, and I'm not ashamed of loving Rupert.'

Mr Lagallan was about to make a retort, when a shout attracted their attention, and a gentleman came trotting towards them on a showy bay hack.

'Lagallan! Well, my good friend, we meet again! And Major Lagallan, is it not? We met at the Meldrums' rout the other night. How do you do, sir?'

Major Lagallan silently inclined his head, and Vivyan forced a small, tight-lipped smile.

'Good day to you, MacCauley. You know my sister-in-law, Mrs Lagallan?'

Mr MacCauley raised his hat, and treated the lady to his wide smile, but his grey eyes were resting all the time on Eustacia.

'This is Miss Marchant,' said Caroline. Mr MacCauley bowed.

'Marchant,' he said, with a slight, interrogatory lift to his brows. 'I don't recognize the name, but I feel sure we have met before.'

'I think it very likely,' put in Caroline, calmly. 'Miss Marchant is staying with Lady Bilderston, and is often seen about the town in my lady's carriage.'

'Ah,' murmured that gentleman, his eyes still fixed upon Eustacia. 'That would be it.'

He stayed beside them a moment longer, exchanged a few more pleasantries with the gentlemen, then rode away. Eustacia cast an anguished glance at Mr Lagallan.

'Oh, Vivyan, I am sure he recognized me!' She saw Caroline's look of surprise and flushed slightly. 'We, um, saw him when we stopped at Reading, on the way to Town.'

Mrs Lagallan threw a startled look at Vivyan, who shook his head at her.

'We exchanged but the merest bow in passing, Caro.'

She did not look convinced, but after a moment she shrugged, and smiled at Eustacia.

'Don't worry, Stacey. You look nothing like the boy Vivyan brought to me.'

'But my hair!' cried Miss Marchant.

'Well, there is that,' admitted Vivyan, 'but even if he did suspect, there is nothing to be gained by it. You can rest easy, child.'

'How do you come to know him, Vivyan?' asked Caroline.

'I had some—er—dealings with him in the past.' He grinned. 'Let us say his past would no

70

more bear investigation than mine own—probably less.'

'Well, he has some entrée into society,' remarked the Major. He smiled at Eustacia. 'However, I think you can put him out of your mind, child. While you are living under the protection of your godmother, even if MacCauley *did* recognize you, he could hardly say so, for who would believe him? Rest easy, child. He cannot hurt you.'

CHAPTER SIX

Miss Marchant found it easy enough to follow the major's advice and forget about Nathan MacCauley, for her days were taken up with numerous fittings for new gowns, and trips to such fascinating shopping-places as the Pantheon Bazaar with Miss Cardwell, her ladyship's dresser, to purchase the gloves, stockings and reticules necessary for any young lady's wardrobe. However, Eustacia did not lose sight of her reason for coming to London, and as each day passed she fretted that she was no closer to finding Rupert Alleyne. Miss Marchant's nature was to act, and the idea of meeting Rupert by chance did not appeal to her, but Lady Bilderston had announced that she should live quietly until she had suitable gowns to wear, so that her entrance into society would be at Lady Trentham's ball, a full week away. Eustacia's impatient spirit chafed at such a delay, and the only outlets for her energies were an occasional drive in the park with her godmama or Mrs Lagallan, and her daily walks with Snuffles, Lady Bilderston's pet spaniel. Taking Snuffles for his morning exercise had very quickly become Eustacia's first task of the day, and because of the proximity of the little railed gardens that gave their name to the area, she was allowed to sally forth unencumbered by a maid or a footman.

*   *   *

It was on one such outing, the morning following her carriage ride with Caroline Lagallan, that the idea first came to Eustacia. As she left the gardens she caught sight of a young couple standing on the corner, closely studying a guidebook. Eustacia halted as a plan began to form itself in her mind, then, with a quickened step, she hurried back to the house, almost dragging Snuffles along with her.

'Avebury,' she addressed the butler as he took the dog's leash and prepared to lead the animal away, 'do we have a guidebook of London in the house?'

'I believe there may be some such thing in the red saloon, Miss.'

'And—and does it contain a street guide, do you think?' she pursued.

'Why yes, Miss, I believe it does. Perhaps you would like me to find it for you?'

'No, no, I will do that myself, while you take Snuffles to the kitchen for a titbit. The red saloon, you said?'

'Yes, Miss. It's on the first floor, and was used to be called the study, when his lordship was alive, and any books we may have will be found there—her ladyship not being much of a reader,' he added, his countenance wooden. 'But if you was wishful to go anywhere in particular, Miss, I am sure one of the footmen would be perfectly able to escort you ...'

'No, no, that will not be necessary, thank you, Avebury.' Eustacia favoured the old retainer with a sweet smile, and made her way upstairs.

The red saloon was a small room tucked away at the back of the house and furnished in an outdated style with heavy, dark furniture, including a large desk. Although the furniture was not shrouded in Holland covers, the room was rarely used, Lady Bilderston preferring to write her letters at the pretty little writing-desk in the morning-room. After several minutes, Eustacia found the guidebook in a large glass-fronted bookcase, and sat down at the desk to study this informative little tome.

She had heard enough from her godmama, and from Mr Lagallan and his brother, to know that the most probable places to find Mr Alleyne during the day would be in the fashionable areas of New Bond Street, the Mall or Piccadilly. She also knew that the gentlemen's clubs most likely to appeal to a young man, such as Brooks's or White's, were in St James's Street. Of course it would not do for her to walk unattended in such a location, but there was no reason why Snuffles should not enjoy an expedition to the Green Park, and it would be an easy matter to slip through one of the adjoining streets to take a peep at St James's Street. Eustacia was well aware that the chances of meeting with Mr Alleyne in these circumstances were slim, but they were certainly greater than if she remained hidden away in Fanshawe Gardens!

*　　　*　　　*

Eager to put her plan into action, Eustacia stepped out the next morning with Snuffles, but instead of heading for the gardens, she turned south and set off for the heart of fashionable London. Snuffles was surprised at this break in routine, but he was happy to trot along beside his young mistress, enjoying the new scents of this hitherto unexplored area. Miss Marchant was anxious not to draw attention to herself, and had chosen for the occasion a demure, dark-green walking-dress and pelisse of impeccable cut but with little ornament, and a close-fitting bonnet to cover her distinctive red hair. Thus attired, and with the guidebook clutched firmly in one hand, she set off on her task in a mood of excited optimism.

*   *   *

New Bond Street was bustling with pedestrians and carriages, and Eustacia made her way through the crowd, confident that it would not be thought improper for an unescorted lady to be walking her dog in such a busy thoroughfare. However, she felt a little less sanguine as she made her way along Piccadilly towards the Green Park, for one fashionably dressed gentleman lifted his eyeglass to study her as she passed him. The starched points of his collar were so high that he was obliged to swivel his whole body to watch her progress, and although at any other time Miss Marchant would have been amused at this behaviour, she began to wonder if it would have been prudent to bring her maid. However, such thoughts were put to flight when she reached the Green Park. The rural setting, complete with a herd of cows, and milkmaids dispensing fresh milk for a small sum, delighted Eustacia. The noise of the busy streets was muted by the trees and bushes that bounded the park, and for a while she could almost imagine that she was at home again in Somerset. But charming as this idea was, she would not let it sway her from her purpose, and she soon slipped out of the park to hurry along a quiet side street. At the junction with St James's Street she stopped, looking up and down the famous thoroughfare, hoping for a glimpse of her quarry. It did not surprise her that Rupert was not in sight, and Miss Marchant consulted her guidebook before hurrying back to the Green Park, determined to try again. It was a fine morning, and the spring sunshine made it a pleasant day for walking. Eustacia was just congratulating herself on her plan when disaster struck.

Snuffles was also enjoying his walk on new territory, and had so far been content to trot along beside Eustacia, but as they walked along Park Place towards St James's Street, a ginger cat that had been sleeping on a sunny wall suddenly caught sight of Snuffles, and took exception to this invasion. The cat, used to leashed dogs parading on the sidewalk below him, arched its back, spitting venomously. Snuffles was a small dog, but there was enough of the wild animal in him to resent such an insult, and he voiced his displeasure by barking loudly. Eustacia scolded him and tugged on the leash, intending to walk on. Snuffles, however, could not ignore the challenge thrown out to him by the ginger tom. He squatted, digging in his heels. Miss Marchant, her attention fixed upon St James's Street, which was but a step ahead of her, gave an impatient tug on the leash.

'Come *on*, Snuffles!'

The leash went slack and, looking down, she saw with dismay that Snuffles had slipped his collar. For a moment, the three participants were frozen into a tableau before the cat realized that its adversary was no longer fettered, and took off along the street, with the spaniel in close pursuit.

'Snuffles!' cried Eustacia, but she knew enough about dogs to be sure he would ignore her. She watched in dismay as the animals raced towards St James's Street, then, with only the smallest hesitation, she picked up her skirts and hurried after them.

*   *   *

Mr Lagallan attributed his habit of rising at an unfashionably early hour to his years adventuring on the Continent. Unable to lie in his bed while his valet brought him coffee or hot chocolate, and then waste another languid hour deciding upon which coat to put on, Vivyan preferred to fill his mornings with physical pursuits such as boxing or fencing. Having spent a profitable hour at small-sword practice with Viscount Denny, the two gentlemen put on their coats and set off from the discreet little duelling-school in King Street to walk to the viscount's lodgings off

77

Piccadilly, where they planned to break their fast. They made their way at a leisurely pace, enjoying the sunshine and discussing plans for the coming day.

'Going to look at Grisham's carriage-horses later,' drawled the viscount, polishing his eyeglass. 'Poor devil's quite done up, you know. Lost everything, apparently, and is selling all his cattle.'

'Is he, by Gad? Carriages, too? Then I've a mind to come along with you, Denny, for he has a very pretty perch-phaeton that would suit me very well.'

The viscount frowned at him.

'Are you sure it's just the phaeton that interests you? I tell you to your head, Viv, I ain't taking you along with me if you are going to bid for his match-bays! I've had my eye on that team for ever, and I'm dashed if I'll let you steal a march on me!'

'No, no, Denny,' said Vivyan, his soothing tones at variance with the gleam in his dark eyes. 'I may cast an eye over the horseflesh, but I've more than enough cattle already eating their heads off in my stables.'

'Dashed if I know why I put up with you,' grumbled the viscount, not at all reassured. 'You'll take a fancy to those bays and outbid me, I know it! And I haven't forgiven you yet for that trick you played me this morning!' he added, with a darkling look at his companion. 'Knocking the blade out of my hand—damned

78

ungentlemanly of you!'

Vivyan laughed, and took his friend's arm as they crossed into St James's Street. 'Denny, you know you were trying to do the same to me! The maestro had just shown us the trick!'

'Aye, only you already knew it!' declared my lord, grinning in spite of himself.

'Well, you will learn it in time. It takes practice. The secret is in the wrist action. I was taught a similar trick by a fencing master in Orleans.'

'Ah, yes. France.' The viscount shook his head. 'You have a sadly chequered past, my friend.'

'I prefer to call it colourful, Denny. Merely colourful.'

The viscount had stopped, and now raised his quizzing-glass.

'As colourful as the stockings adorning those astonishingly pretty ankles across the way?' he drawled.

Vivyan looked up in time to see a small figure in a dark-green pelisse running along the opposite flagway, red hair streaming behind her and skirts held up to display her scarlet stockings.

*   *   *

Eustacia sped on, oblivious to the stares and catcalls that followed her progress. The wind had caught the wide brim of her bonnet and

79

tugged it free of her head, so that it now bounced playfully at her back as she ran. Ahead of her, the ginger cat darted round a corner with Snuffles almost snapping at its tail. Eustacia reached the turning in time to see Snuffles disappearing into one of the alleys that criss-crossed the area behind the fashionable buildings which fronted St James's Street. She hurried on, peering into each alley and calling to the spaniel. When she heard a bark, she knew she was closing in on her quarry, and quickened her step again. As she entered a narrow, cobbled mews she saw two men ahead of her. They were wearing rough workmen's clothing and one was holding a struggling Snuffles under his arm.

'Oh, you have caught my dog—thank you,' she panted, as she approached. 'He slipped his lead, you see.'

'Did 'e now? Well, that was very clever of the little fellow.'

'Perhaps you will hold him while I put his collar around his neck—'

'Not so fast, young miss.' The other man stepped forward, putting up one dirty hand. 'Seems to me we've rescued this dog of yours, and that should be worth somethin', eh, Jacob?'

Eustacia stopped. 'I'm sorry, I do not understand you.'

'Well, it's clear this is a very valuable little animal, and 'is family should be grateful to get 'im back. *Very* grateful, wouldn't you say, Jacob?'

The other man's eyes gleamed, and a black grin split his face.

'Aye, Mack, grateful enough to pay a reward, I do reckon.'

'A reward!' exclaimed Eustacia. 'I am sorry, but I have no money with me.'

'Well, if you ain't got no gelt on ye, then it'll have to be that fine string o' pearls around yer neck . . .'

Anger sparkled in Miss Marchant's eyes.

'My pearls! How dare you? This is blackmail! I insist you hand over my dog immediately.'

'Insist?' declared Jacob. 'You hear that, Mack? The little lady *insists*! It seems she don't want her dog back. But p'raps she'll change 'er mind when he starts to yelp a bit . . .'

Eustacia's flushed cheeks paled. 'You wouldn't hurt a little dog!'

'Oh yes they would, my dear,' drawled a voice at her shoulder. 'But if they value their skins, I think they will give you back your dog now, and unharmed.'

Eustacia spun round to see Mr Lagallan standing behind her, his swordstick drawn from its case and glinting wickedly in the pale sunlight.

The two men stopped grinning.

'We was just 'aving a joke with the lady,' said the one named Jacob, putting Snuffles on

81

the ground and stepping back, his eyes never wavering from the swordstick.

'Aye, we never meant no 'arm,' averred his companion, slowly retreating.

'Then I suggest you go on your way, and we will say no more about the matter.' Vivyan spoke pleasantly, but the swordstick waved gently to and fro before him, a silent menace.

Muttering, the two men turned and hurried away, and had disappeared by the time Eustacia had fastened Snuffles's collar securely about his neck.

'Vivyan, thank you!' she exclaimed, rising and shaking the dust from her skirts. 'I was never more pleased to see anyone in my life— except when I was stuck in a tree, of course!' She smiled up at him, her eyes twinkling. 'You are forever rescuing me.'

'It is becoming a habit! Here, let me hold that leash while you put on your hat. Then I will escort you home.'

'Thank you.' Eustacia retrieved her bonnet, which was hanging behind her, secured only by the ribbons that had knotted about her neck. 'I wore this to cover my hair,' she explained, bundling her tangled locks into the hat's crown. 'But it was not secure, and flew off when I started to run. There—do I look more respectable?'

'A very little!' retorted Vivyan. He handed her the dog-leash and pulled her free hand on to his arm as he escorted her out of the alley.

'I think it would be best if we went this way, into Green Park,' he said. 'It would not do to go back into St James's Street. And perhaps you would like to tell me just what you were doing, running about in that hoydenish fashion?' He glanced down at Snuffles who, exhausted by his exertions, was trotting along quietly at Eustacia's heels. 'But perhaps I can guess most of it.'

'Well, there was a cat.'

'Ah. Then, of course, everything becomes clear.'

'It hissed at Snuffles, and he slipped his collar and chased after it.'

'Naturally,' said Vivyan, solemnly.

'Well, it *is* natural for dogs to chase cats,' argued Miss Marchant. 'What could I do? I could not leave Godmama's pet to lose itself in these streets. I was obliged to run after him.'

'Through St James's Street?'

'That was unfortunate,' she conceded, 'but since so few people know me yet, perhaps it is not so very bad.'

'That may be true, but I, on the other hand, am extremely well-known, and I was obliged to race after you. Pray spare a thought for *my* reputation.'

Miss Marchant stopped and looked up at her escort, anxiously scanning his face. Then, seeing the amused gleam in his dark eye, she relaxed.

'Oh, were you on the strut, sir?' she asked

him, innocently. 'I had no idea you were a—a *Bond Street beau.* It would, of course, accord ill with your status to be seen running.'

'No, my sweet saucepot, I am not a Bond Street beau, and it will accord ill with my status to be seen strangling you, but that event will very likely come to pass if I have any more of your insolence!'

Eustacia laughed, and squeezed his arm.

'I am so glad you were at hand to rescue me, Vivyan! It was very wrong of me to bring Snuffles so far from his home, and I am cross with myself for not checking his collar was secure, but thank you for not scolding me, and telling me how foolish I have been, for I am very well aware of it, I assure you, and could not be more sorry!'

'And may one enquire why you were in that vicinity in the first place, brat?'

Eustacia bit her lip.

'I—I was looking for Rupert. I did not mean to go down the street at all,' she hurried on. 'I was walking Snuffles here in the Green Park, but the guidebook showed me several roads leading through to St James's Street, so I thought I could walk as far as the corner and . . . and *look,* just in case Rupert should be in sight. And everything was going so well, until we came upon that cat! Vivyan, do—do you think I have done irreparable damage to my reputation?'

He suppressed a grin.

'Not irreparable, my dear, but that carrot-top of yours is distinctive. Fortunately, you have lived very secluded, so few people will recognize you, and it is to be hoped that when Lady Bilderston introduces you into society, no one will connect the decorous Miss Marchant with the red-haired minx seen racing through town today. When is your first party?'

'Five days' time. Lady Trentham's ball.'

'Five days—a lifetime! Don't fret, my little nymph, anyone who saw you today will surely have forgotten the incident by then!'

Miss Marchant was not so confident, but she said nothing of her adventures to Lady Bilderston, and even found the escapade fading from her mind as preparations for her first outing into society drew near.

*   *   *

On the evening of the Trentham ball, Miss Marchant stood before her mirror, gazing in wonder at her reflection. 'Godmama, it is perfect!'

Lady Bilderston smiled over her shoulder.

'The gown is very beautiful, and so are you, my love.' Eustacia turned, tears making her eyes shine an even deeper green.

'How am I ever to repay you for all you have done for me? This gown is twice as grand as anything I have ever had before—better even than the gown Aunt Jayne chose for my presentation!' She smoothed her hands over the material. The thin silver gauze hung like gossamer over the underdress of green satin, dainty green slippers peeped out from the edge of her skirts, and Cardwell had presented her with a pair of green gloves to complete her toilet. An emerald ribbon was threaded through the red-gold curls, and Lady Bilderston herself was obliged to blink away a tear.

'Now, don't cry, my love,' she said, patting Eustacia's hands. 'You don't want to make those pretty eyes of yours red. Eliza—Lady Trentham—is a very good friend of mine, and the world and his wife will be filling her salons tonight, so it is important that you are looking your best. Do you know, I am enjoying your visit much more than I ever thought I would, and I am very glad I had Celeste make up this gown for you. I am sure that your Aunt Jayne is an admirable creature, but when your trunks arrived, and I saw those abominable pinks she had chosen to trick you out in—and with your colouring, too! It was no wonder you did not *take* when she presented you.'

Miss Marchant's eyes twinkled mischievously.

'But Godmama, everyone knows that pink and white are the *only* colours for a débutante!'

'Aye, if she's a brunette!' came the retort. 'They serve only to make your complexion look sallow. No, we were very right to pack them all away, and I have told Celeste she must have at least three more of your gowns ready by next week.'

'Oh, Godmama!' Eustacia hugged her ruthlessly. 'I feel just like Cinderella!'

Lady Bilderston gave a fat chuckle.

'Well then, my dear, the carriage will be at the door at any moment: let us get you to the ball before all your finery turns back to rags!'

CHAPTER SEVEN

Trentham House was already full when they arrived, and, glancing at the coaches lined up behind them, Eustacia wondered how they would ever fit so many guests into the house. Their hostess was an old friend of Lady Bilderston's and she greeted them with a triumphant smile.

'Such a dreadful squeeze, my dears, I declare we shall be excessively uncomfortable. It will be such a success!'

Miss Marchant was a little awed by so many strangers, but her spirits lifted when she spotted Major Lagallan and his wife across the room. Making a mental note to seek them out later, she gave her attention to the young man being introduced to her, and as he led her on to the dance-floor, she forgot her own nervousness and attempted to put him at his ease. Lady Bilderston nodded and smiled her encouragement, and went off to join her friends for a cosy gossip, confident that her young charge would not be without a partner for the best part of the evening.

*   *   *

When Mr Lagallan arrived, shortly before eleven, he found Eustacia in high spirits. During a break in the dancing, he made his way towards her.

'Well, Miss Marchant, are you enjoying yourself?'

The glowing face that was turned towards him gave him his answer. He grinned.

'I suppose I am too late to claim a dance with you?'

'Heavens, yes. I am engaged for every dance! But you can expect nothing else if you will arrive so late!'

'Shrew!'

Her eyes sparkled.

'No, how can that be when I am merely telling the truth? But, Vivyan, tell me honestly—do you like my gown?'

She stepped back, spreading her skirts and twirling before him. Vivyan grinned inwardly as those nearest raised their brows: it would seem Miss Marchant was unaware that fashionable young ladies should never display such enthusiasm at a party!

'It is very beautiful, don't you think? Godmama had it made up for me.'

He raised his glass to study her. 'Very fetching.'

'Is that the best you can do?' she demanded. 'You should know, sir, that I have received some very fine compliments this evening.'

'I'll wager you have, you abominable brat! Very well, you look like . . .'

She waited expectantly, her ready smile hovering on her lips.

'A frost-coated plant.'

She gave a gurgle of laughter, and put one hand up to her red curls.

'A marigold, perhaps, or even a carrot! Look, my partner approaches for the next dance, so I leave you, Mr Lagallan.' She tossed her head, her eyes dancing. 'You do not deserve that I should talk to you!'

Smiling, he watched her skip away to join the next set, and wandered off in search of refreshment.

*   *   *

After two energetic dances, Miss Marchant left her partner and went to find her godmother. As she pushed her way through the crowded rooms, she came upon Mr Lagallan. He was talking to a willowy young lady in a gown of celestial blue. Eustacia hesitated, not wanting to intrude, but even as she began to turn away she heard Mr Lagallan addressing her, and she turned back, smiling.

'Pray, do not let me interrupt you.'

'No, no, we were just talking of you.' Mr Lagallan's dark eyes gleamed wickedly. 'You know Miss Pensford, I believe?'

'Of course, we are neighbours,' the tall young lady affirmed, turning her blue eyes upon Miss Marchant. 'How do you do, Eustacia? I had no idea you would be in Town.'

'N-no. My godmama invited me, at short notice.'

Miss Pensford's gaze rested on Eustacia's flushed countenance.

'You are heated from your dancing. How thoughtless of me to keep you standing here. Perhaps Mr Lagallan would procure some lemonade for us?'

Vivyan bowed. 'Of course. I will leave you two ladies to enjoy a little gossip!'

Smiling, Miss Pensford linked her arm with Eustacia's and led her to an empty sofa.

'I wish you had written to tell me you were in Town, we could have met earlier.'

'It—it was very much a surprise when Godmama invited me to join her, it was very unexpected.' That much at least is true, thought Eustacia. 'But what of you, Helen? I thought you were to remain at Combe Charlton until the New Year.'

'And so we were, but—circumstances

changed.' A faint blush suffused Miss Pensford's pale cheek. 'Papa decided we had been in deep mourning long enough—it was not a very close relative, after all—and we have lived very retired at Combe Charlton these past months. Mama is not yet wearing colours, of course, but she thought it would not be unseemly to bring me to Town. Of course, we shall only attend a few select parties.' Remembering the press of people in every room, Eustacia thought privately that Lady Trentham's ball could scarcely be considered a *select* party. Miss Pensford's gaze rested again upon Eustacia. 'How is it you know Mr Lagallan?'

'Oh, his—his sister-in-law, Mrs Philip Lagallan, escorted me to town.' Eustacia held her breath, but her answer seemed to satisfy her companion, who merely smiled.

'He is very agreeable, is he not?'

'I—I hardly know him,' muttered Eustacia, feeling very uncomfortable.

Miss Pensford's smile grew. 'We met last season, and when we stood up together everyone said what a handsome couple we made.' She lowered her voice, leaning closer to her companion. 'He visited Papa at Combe Charlton a few weeks ago, and we came to an *understanding.* Nothing has been announced, of course, for Papa thought it would be best to wait a little while, for we do not wish to offend our dear cousin's family by appearing to cut short our mourning, but still, I am sure it must be all over the county by now, so I can see no harm in you knowing.'

'Th-thank you. I wish you very happy.'

Miss Pensford unfurled her fan.

'I have no doubt we shall be; it is a very good match.'

'But I thought your mama wanted you to marry a title!' Eustacia flushed. 'Oh, my wretched tongue! I beg your pardon!'

'No, no, you are quite right, but when we considered the matter last season, they were all so unsuitable! Most were older than Papa, and the rest were looking for a rich wife to repair their fortunes or were of such unsavoury character that Papa would not countenance them, whatever their rank.'

Miss Marchant stared. 'And—and your Papa considered Mr Lagallan's character sufficiently unblemished?'

Eustacia found herself subjected to a puzzled look.

'But of course! There was a little wildness in his youth, I believe, but that was many years ago. His character now is impeccable.'

Miss Marchant was silenced; the object of their discussion was approaching, and she could only be relieved that she was spared the necessity of a reply—she was well aware that her unruly tongue might lead her into impropriety.

'Well, ladies, have you had sufficient time to

cover every possible topic of conversation?'

'Not at all,' said Miss Pensford, smiling. 'As a matter of fact we have discussed very little— in the main, yourself.'

'Oh? And have you comprehensively destroyed my character?'

Eustacia, in the act of sipping her lemonade, choked, but Helen replied seriously, 'That would be most improper. I was merely curious to know how it is that you and Eustacia are acquainted.'

'I explained that Caroline had brought me to town,' put in Stacey, hurriedly. She found herself growing hot under Mr Lagallan's quizzing gaze, and, feeling that she had had quite enough teasing for one night, she excused herself and moved off into the crowd to seek Lady Bilderston.

*   *   *

Eustacia was about to make her way downstairs to the supper-room when a familiar voice brought her to a halt. She turned towards the small chamber that had been set aside for cards: standing just inside the doorway was a group of gentlemen, and Eustacia fixed her eyes on the young man nearest the door. He had his back to her, but she took in the guinea-gold curls, brushed into fashionable disorder, the familiar line of his back, the shapely legs encased in black knee-breeches.

'Rupert!' Her cry was scarcely above a whisper. She tried to compose herself. 'M-Mr Alleyne?'

The gentleman turned, and Eustacia forced her knees not to give way at the sight of his handsome face. The blue eyes that rested upon her widened in surprise, but the gentleman made a quick recovery.

'Miss Marchant.' He bowed to her. 'But how is this? I thought you were in Somerset.'

He did not appear overjoyed to see her, but Stacey realized how surprised he must be to find her in London.

'I am staying with my godmother, Lady Bilderston—Fanshawe Gardens,' she added.

'Ah. I see.' He nodded and smiled, and Eustacia waited, smiling up at him and taking in every feature of his dear face.

'You did not expect to find me here.'

'No—that is—'

'Are you not pleased to see me, Rupert?'

'Oh, of course. Delighted.'

Her smile wavered, and she thought he looked anything but delighted to see her.

'Miss Marchant, your godmama has sent me to find you.' She looked up to find Vivyan beside her. He drew her hand on to his arm, smiling down at her.

'Lady Bilderston awaits you in the supper-room. I am come to take you to her.' He turned towards Mr Alleyne. 'If you will excuse us, sir?'

Succumbing to the pressure of his fingers, Eustacia moved away.

'That was your Rupert, I presume?' Vivyan guided her down the shallow staircase.

'Y—yes.' Eustacia did not want to talk. The meeting had not been the joyous occasion she had imagined.

'You surprised him, I've no doubt.'

She turned to look at Vivyan.

'Yes. Yes, I *did* surprise him, didn't I?' She looked up at him, her eyes begging him for reassurance. Vivyan patted her hand.

'Of course.' He smiled grimly. 'You gave him quite a shock.'

*   *   *

Miss Marchant was unusually quiet during supper, a fact which Lady Bilderston ascribed to tiredness. However, a suggestion that they should leave early was vehemently refused. Casting her mind back over her meeting with Rupert, Miss Marchant was soon convinced that her sudden appearance had momentarily overpowered that young man. Now that the initial surprise was over she did not doubt that he would seek her out, that they would return to the easy intimacy they had shared in Somerset. She blushed a little at the memory of Mr Alleyne's whispered endearments, and the secret kisses they had enjoyed. Of course, they would have to be more circumspect, but there was no reason why they should not see each other regularly in London.

When the dancing resumed, Eustacia accompanied her godmother back to the ballroom, her heart jumping with excitement, but there was no sign of Mr Alleyne. She glanced into the card-room as they passed—he was not there. Screwing up her courage, she approached one of the young men she had seen earlier with Rupert.

'Mr Alleyne? Why, he's gone, ma'am. Left while you was at supper, I dare say. Something about a previous engagement.'

Miss Marchant walked slowly back into the ballroom. The orchestra was striking up again but she excused herself to her partner and moved away to a vacant sofa to gather her thoughts. Across the room, Vivyan watched her. He noted the pale cheek, the faint crease in her brow, and went to sit beside her.

'What's this, not dancing, Stacey?'

'What? Oh, no, I have had enough of dancing for this evening.'

'And where is Mr Alleyne?'

Eustacia put up her chin.

'Rupert?' she said, with studied carelessness. 'Oh, I don't know—gone, I think.'

'I see.'

'Yes. A—a previous engagement.'

'Of course.'

After a pause, she forced herself to

converse.

'Where is Miss Pensford?'

'Dancing with some young buck. She thinks it would be wrong for us to spend the entire evening together until we are formally engaged.'

'I had not expected to see Helen in Town.'

'No more had I! When I left Combe Charlton, I thought they were settled there for the winter.'

'I think Mr Pensford has brought Helen to Town to keep an eye upon his investment,' observed Miss Marchant.

'You mean myself?'

'Of course.' She chuckled. 'Helen considers your character to be impeccable.'

'The devil she does! Well then, I had better not sit here with you for too long, or it will ruin both our reputations! Do you drive out with Caroline tomorrow?'

She instantly became serious.

'No. I shall be at home tomorrow. Rupert may call, and I must not miss him.'

*　　　*　　　*

But Mr Alleyne did not call at Fanshawe Gardens the following day, nor any other day that week, and it was not until Lady Beasley's rout that Eustacia saw him again.

She was standing alone at one side of the room when Mr Alleyne came in, and her hostess, observing Eustacia's anxious look, brought the young gentleman to her, making it impossible for him to do other than ask her to dance.

As they took their places on the dance-floor, Eustacia glanced up at her partner and, observing that he looked a little uncomfortable, asked him bluntly if he was not pleased to see her.

'P-pleased? Of course I am, Miss Marchant,' stammered Mr Alleyne, flushing. 'It's just that—'

Eustacia felt hot tears stinging her eyelids.

'If you don't love me, Rupert, pray tell me so at once.'

'No, that's not it! I mean—dash it all, Stacey, I can't talk about it here, in the midst of all these people!'

'Then where?'

Mr Alleyne cast about in his mind. 'Tomorrow, somewhere . . .'

'There's a little park in Fanshawe Gardens, where I walk Godmama's little dog. I could be there tomorrow morning, if you like.'

Mr Alleyne swallowed nervously.

'Well . . .' He looked down to find a pair of trusting green eyes raised to his, and his courage failed him. 'Very well—eleven o'clock.'

CHAPTER EIGHT

For Eustacia, the next twelve hours seemed interminable. She woke soon after dawn and tried to curb her excitement. At 10.30 she collected Snuffles, and dragged the little animal out for his morning walk. By eleven o'clock she was already in the park, anxiously looking out for Mr Alleyne. He arrived ten minutes late, by which time Eustacia was so overwrought that she threw herself against him, crying, 'Oh, Rupert, I have missed you so!'

Mr Alleyne, aghast at this public display, held her away from him, and begged her to be a little more circumspect.

'But I love you, and I have come all the way to London to tell you so!'

'That is very good of you, Stacey, but—I told you when I left Somerset that it cannot be.'

She clutched his hands.

'But I do not understand! I am not quite a pauper, you know! I thought that if we were to face your father together, and tell him that we love each other, he could be persuaded to let us marry.'

Mr Alleyne gazed down helplessly at the little face upturned to his. He was not a cruel young man, although a childhood indulged by doting parents had made him thoughtless. A series of ill-placed bets and the importunities of his tailor had made it necessary for him to withdraw from London the previous summer to await his next quarter's allowance, and he had chosen to pay a long-overdue visit to his uncle at Burnett Lodge, where he had whiled away his enforced rustication by conducting a heady flirtation with the prettiest young lady in the area. That Miss Marchant had fallen head over heels in love with him had not worried the young man at all, and when it was time to return to London he had made his excuses and left Somerset and Eustacia with no regrets, salving the very minute pricking of his conscience with the thought that, although she might shed a few tears for him, she would soon recover and settle down to happily married life as the wife of some country squire.

But Mr Alleyne was a poor judge of character, and he had not understood the depth of Eustacia's feelings for him, nor her determination. His excuse for leaving Somerset had been that his father wanted him to marry an heiress, and even now, with Miss Marchant's gaze turned so trustingly to his own, he could not bring himself to tell her the truth. With an exasperated sigh, he ran a hand through his elegantly pomaded locks.

'Oh, Stacey, you are such an innocent, you don't understand these things.'

She gazed up at him lovingly. 'Don't fret,

my love. Now we are together I am confident we can find a way to persuade your papa. When may I meet him?'

Mr Alleyne felt the ground being cut away from beneath his feet.

'He—he's out of town at present.'

'Oh, that is too bad! But it does not matter, we shall just have to be patient. Having travelled all this way, I am not to be daunted by such a little set-back.'

'Yes, and that reminds me, just how *did* you get to London?'

'Oh, Rupert, it was such an adventure!' Eustacia declared, her eyes shining. 'I told Grandpapa I would be staying with my old governess for a few weeks, then I borrowed a suit of boy's clothes and set off to catch the mail from Bath.'

Mr Alleyne regarded her with horror. 'Alone? Dressed as a boy? Stacey, you did not!'

'No, as a matter of fact I *didn't*!' she retorted, her elation dying in the face of his disapproval. 'Mrs Lagallan came upon me, and—and persuaded me to travel with her.'

'She would have served you better had she sent you home again!'

'Rupert, how can you say so? How else was I to find you?'

At that moment, Snuffles chose to take exception to a well-bred poodle walking in the opposite direction. Eustacia gave her attention to the spaniel, pulling him up sharply, and thus did not see Mr Alleyne's hunted expression. By the time Snuffles had finished uttering his challenge and was again walking quietly beside Eustacia, the young man had gathered his wits.

'Stacey—Miss Marchant! My—my behaviour in Somerset was perhaps a little . . . reprehensible. It would not do for us to conduct ourselves quite so—so *freely* here in Town.'

'Oh, I am quite aware of that,' came the sunny reply. 'I do not expect you to stand up with me for every dance, nor would I want you to live in my pocket—'

Mr Alleyne frowned. 'A most unladylike term,' he muttered repressively, 'but you are right, and there must be no more meetings such as this—it is not at all the thing!'

'B—but Rupert, I thought you wanted to see me!'

'I do, of course, but I would not have any scandal attached to us—to you.'

Miss Marchant put her hand on his arm and smiled up mistily at him.

'How very thoughtful you are, Rupert. I do love you!'

He flushed. 'Yes, well—I'd better leave you now. It wouldn't do for people to see us together.'

'When will I see you?'

'Oh, I don't know—that is—'

'You could call upon Godmama.'

'No! I mean, I would much rather wait until

I have been formally introduced to Lady Bilderston; no need to rush these things. Look, you will be at the Mayfields' ball, won't you? I shall ensure I make Lady Bilderston's acquaintance then.'

'But that is days away—can we not meet before?'

Patiently, Mr Alleyne explained again why it would be imprudent for them to meet too often, and he took his leave, praying that something would occur to prevent him attending the Mayfields' ball.

*   *   *

Mr Alleyne was not the only gentleman reluctant to appear at this prestigious event. Mr Lagallan was dining at Bruton Street when his sister-in-law asked him if he meant to attend.

'Lord, yes, I suppose I must. Helen made it plain that she expects me to be there.'

Major Lagallan's lips twitched. He said with mock severity: 'That is not very complimentary to your future bride.'

Vivyan grinned. 'Shocking, ain't it? I thought myself free from this sort of thing for a few more months yet. When I went to Combe Charlton to propose to Helen, I was told the family was still in mourning for some sort of cousin. That's why there's to be no announcement about the engagement yet.

Then, without a word, the whole family is in Town!'

'To keep a watchful eye on you, perhaps,' murmured Caroline. 'You are something of a prize, you know.'

Mr Lagallan raised his brows. 'Do they think that I would cry off, when I have already agreed everything with Helen and her father?'

'Put down those hackles, little brother,' said the Major, grinning, 'no one is doubting your intentions. It's understandable that Miss Pensford should wish you to attend her.'

'Aye,' agreed Vivyan gloomily, 'and unless I break a leg or some such thing, I suppose I shall have to do so!'

*   *   *

Since no mishap occurred in the following days, Mr Lagallan dutifully presented himself in Earl Mayfield's crowded ballroom in good time to lead Miss Pensford on to the floor for the first two dances. He was also able to secure one dance with Eustacia, and as they took their places in the set he complimented her upon her glowing looks. She did indeed look very well in a flowing gown of green lustring, with a single string of fine pearls gleaming at her neck. He regarded her closely, but could detect no hint of reserve or unhappiness beneath her sparkling good humour.

'You have spoken to Mr Alleyne?'

Immediately her smile widened.

'Yes. We talked a few days ago. Of course you will understand that he cannot constantly be in attendance upon me, for that would arouse the sort of gossip and speculation that is most abhorrent to us.'

'I thought it was the world well lost with you,' observed Vivyan.

Miss Marchant flushed slightly. 'Well, it is, but Rupert does not wish any scandal to be attached to our liaison.'

The movement of the dance separated them, and they did not mention Mr Alleyne again until the dance had ended, and Vivyan was escorting Miss Marchant off the dance-floor. She cast a shy glance up at him.

'Would you—that is—I should very much like to introduce Mr Alleyne to you, if you could allow it?'

'Of course. Whatever made you think I should object?'

She gave her head a little shake. 'I'm not sure. I think perhaps it is that you sound a little . . . disapproving when we talk of Rupert.'

Taken aback by her perspicacity, Mr Lagallan stifled any misgivings he felt about the young man, and smiled down at his companion.

'Not a bit, Stacey! I should be delighted to meet him.'

*   *   *

105

It was midway through the evening before Mr Alleyne made an appearance. Eustacia was in the ante-room, standing near one of the tall windows with Helen Pensford, when she saw Mr Alleyne coming towards her. Immediately she broke off her conversation, her face lighting up as the young gentleman approached.

'At last you are here, Rupert! I had almost given you up!' She held out her hand to him.

Mr Alleyne bowed over her hand.

'My apologies, Miss Marchant.' He stressed her name, as if to chastise her for her own outspoken address. 'I am sorry I am so late, I—' The words died on his lips as he raised his eyes and looked for the first time upon Eustacia's companion. Miss Pensford had been standing with her back to him as he approached, but now he was aware of the full force of her beauty. He was immediately struck by the contrast between the two young ladies: Eustacia's flaming red hair and sparkling vivacity threw into strong relief Miss Pensford's cool ivory colouring. She was dressed in a gown of cream satin, which hung in soft folds about her willowy figure. Her corn-coloured hair was decorated with delicate white rose-buds, and her flawless skin was accentuated by the cornflower blue of her eyes, whose glance now rested upon Mr Alleyne with a look of cool friendliness. Mr

Alleyne had not been an attentive scholar, but he was suddenly reminded of an ice-maiden from some half-forgotten classical myth.

Watching this little tableau, Miss Marchant was unsurprised. She and Helen had attended many assemblies together in Somerset, and she was well aware of the effect of that cool beauty on young men. If she was disappointed that Rupert should succumb quite so readily to these charms, she stifled such ignoble feelings and performed the introduction, and after allowing them a few moments' conversation, she plucked at Mr Alleyne's sleeve.

'Rupert, the orchestra is striking up again, and I have saved this next dance for you.'

Reluctantly, Mr Alleyne tore himself away from Miss Pensford and accompanied Eustacia to the ballroom.

'Miss Pensford is a neighbour of yours in Somerset, Stacey? I do not recall seeing her when I was at Burnett Lodge.'

'Her family had just suffered a bereavement, and were living very retired.'

'Ah, I see. But she is out of mourning now, I suppose, and will be in London for the season?'

'Perhaps, I do not know,' Eustacia replied, briefly. She found his interest in her friend disturbing, and was relieved that the movement of the dance prevented further discussion.

The rest of the evening passed off as Eustacia had planned, but as the coach carried her back to Fanshawe Gardens in the early hours of the morning, she was aware of a faint cloud of disappointment settling over her. She could not say why this should be: Rupert had danced with her twice, and even had she wished to dance more with him it would have been impossible, since there had been a gratifying number of partners vying for her attention. She had been a little surprised to see Mr Alleyne standing up with Helen Pensford, for that beauty never lacked partners, and surely Rupert had arrived too late to secure a dance. Eustacia had been pleased when Mr Alleyne was introduced to Lady Bilderston, and even if she was a little disappointed that he did not make an appointment to call, that was not sufficient excuse for the lowness of spirits that had settled over her, and in the darkness of the carriage she went over the evening in her mind, trying to find a reason for her depression.

It seemed to begin from the moment she had presented Mr Alleyne to Vivyan. The two gentlemen had been perfectly civil; in fact Mr Lagallan had been at his most charming and had even invited Rupert to accompany him to his club. Eustacia had been a little surprised at this, since she guessed that there must be ten years separating the two men. But she smiled at Mr Lagallan, grateful for this gesture, and as he moved away he paused beside her.

'Well, nymph,' he murmured quietly, 'you have your man now, you no longer need me. I will bid you goodbye.'

Sitting in the darkness of the coach, with Lady Bilderston snoring gently beside her, Eustacia frowned over the remark. Vivyan had left soon after, so there had been no chance to ask him what he meant by it, but she did not see that their friendship should change merely because she had found Rupert.

*   *   *

The following morning, Eustacia's youthful spirits were fully restored by a few hours' sleep. She had formed the habit of walking Snuffles every morning in the little park at one end of Fanshawe Gardens. Lady Bilderston allowed her to dispense with the services of an escort for these excursions, and Eustacia, accustomed to the freedom of long country walks, had come to value these morning outings as a period of solitude in her crowded days.

The previous night's assembly had caused her to sleep a little later that morning, and it was almost noon when she set out with Snuffles for the park. Once inside the gates, she bent to unfasten the little dog's lead, and

109

as she straightened she heard someone call her name. Looking around, she saw a gentleman striding towards her, and her heart sank as she recognized Nathan MacCauley.

'Miss Marchant! Well, well, this is a pleasant surprise!' Mr MacCauley took off his hat and swept her a low bow, his fair hair falling forward over his brow as he rose. 'I stepped out to take the air and—may I have the pleasure of accompanying you?'

Eustacia hesitated. She had no maid with her, but she was not alarmed, for the little park was not empty: several nursemaids from the surrounding houses had brought their charges to the park to take advantage of the fine autumn morning. With a slight inclination of her head, she allowed Mr MacCauley to fall into step beside her.

'I am pleased to have this opportunity to renew our acquaintance, Miss Marchant. As you know, I am a friend of Mr Lagallan's, a great friend.' He glanced down at his companion, but when she remained silent he continued: 'Yes, our friendship goes back a very long way. How long have you known Vivyan?'

'Not long,' she replied, cautiously. 'Only since coming to London.'

'Ah yes, Vivyan escorted you to Town, did he not?'

Eustacia forced herself not to look up at him.

'No, I travelled here with Mrs Lagallan,' she said firmly.

'You are related to Mrs Lagallan, perhaps, some sort of cousin?'

'No, she is a very good friend of—of my family.'

'And where did you say your family live?'

'I did not.' Eustacia quickened her pace.

'Oh, of course, of course.'

They walked on in silence, and Eustacia hoped that her snub would quell her companion's desire to talk, but soon he began again. However, this time his conversation was so innocuous that she began to relax, and he even succeeded in making her laugh. Even so, she was relieved when she had completed her circuit and was again at the park gates. She secured Snuffles once more on his lead, and bade Mr MacCauley good day, but he insisted upon escorting her to her door, his manner perfectly polite, yet once inside the house and alone, Eustacia could not settle, and when Mrs Lagallan called to take her out that afternoon, she could scarcely wait until they reached the park before relating the whole episode to her.

'Caroline, I am sure he has guessed the truth!' she ended, wringing her hands in dismay. 'There was such a knowing look in his eye!'

'My dear, what can he do if he *has* guessed? As Philip has said, no one would believe such a tale! Just hold firm to our story, my love, and we shall come about.'

Miss Marchant knew this to be very good advice, but she was still thankful that Nathan MacCauley was rarely to be seen at the parties she attended with her godmama.

*   *   *

In fact, Mr MacCauley was finding life in town much harder than he had expected. He had used his modest fortune to set himself up in style, taking rooms off Piccadilly, ordering his clothes from the most fashionable tailors, and generally posing as a smart man about town. The only cloud on his horizon was his lack of useful acquaintances.

He found himself living on the fringes of society, without the necessary entrée to the homes of London's top hostesses where, he was sure, his charm and wit could be truly appreciated. He bought himself a showy hack and rode in the park at the appointed hour, strolled down Bond Street with all the other beaux, but still only managed to get himself invited to one or two of the lesser drawing-rooms. As he fretted over his singular lack of success, he convinced himself that he could lay the blame for this failure squarely at Mr Lagallan's door.

Vivyan Lagallan was the darling of society: his fortune could only be described as comfortable, but his striking good looks and polished manners made him a favourite with the hostesses who considered that his presence added lustre to their parties. Mr MacCauley thought it would have cost Vivyan very little to introduce his old friend to these same hostesses, and he had but thought it a great stroke of good fortune to meet Vivyan in Reading; but Mr Lagallan's blunt refusal to help him had been a shock, and it was not long before his disappointment was replaced by anger. Of course he was grateful to Vivyan for coming to his aid when he had been set upon by his pugilistic acquaintances, but nevertheless Nathan MacCauley considered that there was something havey-cavey about the young cousin whom Vivyan had in tow, and once he had seen Vivyan and Miss Marchant together, he was pretty sure he had rumbled him. However, he did not see how this information could be used to his advantage, since any attempt to discredit Vivyan would almost inevitably rebound. No, thought Mr MacCauley, he could not see his way clear yet, but Eustacia Marchant was a pretty little thing, and he had no objection to furthering his acquaintance with her, since Mr Lagallan's door was so firmly closed against him.

CHAPTER NINE

Once Rupert Alleyne had been made known to Lady Bilderston, Miss Marchant was eager to further this acquaintance, and when she spotted an advertisement during one of her shopping trips with her godmother, she realized she had found a perfect opportunity. She waited until Lady Bilderston was settled once more in the carriage before saying casually:

'Godmama, there is a masquerade evening at Vauxhall Gardens next week. I wonder—do you think we could get up a small party?'

Lady Bilderston smiled at her.

'My dear child, with all the balls, routs and ridottos we have attended, have you not had enough of parties?'

'But Godmama, I have heard so much about the gardens—the thousands of coloured lamps, the orchestra playing in the Quadrangle, the Cascade—I would so dearly love to go!'

'But Stacey, it is not at all fashionable now, you know—'

'Perhaps not, but I heard Lady Trentham telling you that she had gone there recently, and found it most diverting!'

Lady Bilderston could not deny it, and, faced with her god-daughter's entreaties, she soon found herself agreeing to the scheme.

'And who would you like me to invite to join us?' she asked Miss Marchant.

'Well, I thought perhaps Miss Pensford might join us.'

'A very pretty-behaved young lady,' approved my lady, who was beginning to warm to the idea. 'And I think I shall invite Colonel Brentwood. Now, pray don't frown so, Stacey. I know you may think him a little old, but he has been my good friend for many years, and besides, we shall require a gentleman to escort us.'

'I—I was thinking that p-perhaps we could invite Mr Alleyne,' muttered Eustacia, hoping that her godmother would not notice her flushed cheeks.

'We can, of course: that will give us five people,' said Lady Bilderston, counting them off on her fingers. 'The supper-boxes will hold six comfortably, so perhaps we should ask another gentleman, just to make up the numbers. Do you think Mr Lagallan might come along? He is a friend of Miss Pensford's, I believe.'

But when the invitations were issued, the messenger brought back Mr Lagallan's reply immediately: unfortunately that gentleman was already engaged elsewhere.

'Now, that *is* regrettable,' declared Lady Bilderston, handing the note to Eustacia. 'Can you think of any other young gentleman who might fill the gap?'

Miss Marchant confessed that she could not, and after a few moments' contemplation her godmother gave a sigh, and shook her head.

'No more can I. We shall have to go as we are. I am sure Mr Alleyne will be able to entertain two young ladies without any trouble!'

Miss Marchant informed Rupert of this treat when they met at the subscription ball at Almack's the following Wednesday, and was surprised at his lack of enthusiasm.

'What is the matter, Rupert, do you not wish to see Vauxhall?'

'As a matter of fact I have been there, several times,' admitted the young man. 'But—Vauxhall is—can be—a little rowdy. It is not at all good *ton*, you know.'

'But Rupert, everyone goes there! And what harm can there be in it? Godmama will make sure we come to no harm. Besides,' she added, her eyes twinkling, 'we shall be masked, so no one will recognize us.'

'Aye, 'tis the disguise that can sometimes make perfectly respectable people behave most improperly!' he muttered darkly.

Eustacia laughed at him.

'Oh, Rupert, do you think Helen and I will turn into hoydens just because our faces are covered?'

'I have no doubt Miss Pensford would never

116

allow herself to overstep propriety,' he returned stiffly, 'but you, Stacey—your liveliness can sometimes lead you to go too far.'

'You did not object to it in Somerset!' she flashed, an angry flush mounting her cheeks.

Mr Alleyne looked away.

'No, and I have already told you how much I regret that episode.'

He left her soon after, and Eustacia realized with a sinking heart that she had never felt so out of charity with him, as she confessed to Mr Lagallan when they met in the park the following day.

Eustacia was riding a lively grey mare—a present from Lady Bilderston, and the horse's fine hocks, beautiful action and excellent lineage had to be discussed before anything else, but a chance word from Mr Lagallan made Eustacia enquire anxiously if perhaps she should ask her godmama to cancel the visit to Vauxhall.

'Good God, no! Why should you want to do that, nymph? The last time we met, you could talk of nothing else.'

'Oh, I know! And I do really want to go, to see the Cascade, and the Dark Walk, and—and everything!'

'But?'

'Well, *you* declined to come with us.'

He looked amused. 'Only because I have a prior engagement.'

'But you have been to the gardens before, and—and you see nothing wrong with our going?'

'Not at all. Why should I?'

She bit her lip, then blurted out, 'Rupert is afraid that—that the masks will be a cover for indiscretion!'

'I am sure they will be, in some instances,' replied Mr Lagallan, his eyes dancing. 'Is Mr Alleyne afraid you might allow yourself to be . . . indiscreet?'

She nodded, indignation once more colouring her cheeks.

'He deplores my liveliness, and thinks it may lead me to behave with—with impropriety!'

'Not that you would ever do such a thing.'

Her brow cleared and she laughed. 'Of course I would not, under normal circumstances! I am surprised Mrs Pensford will allow her daughter to accompany me, if I am such a bad influence!'

He grinned at her. 'Oh, I don't think even you could lead Helen astray!'

'But it will spoil the evening if Rupert is going to disapprove of everything!'

'My dear child, has your godmama invited any ineligible persons to join you?'

She sighed. 'No, that is just it. It is to be the most unexceptional party. Lady Bilderston has asked Colonel Brentwood to accompany us—do you know him? He is extremely old, and very deaf, but he dotes upon Godmama, and she thinks an older male escort is essential. Then there are only Miss Pensford, Mr Alleyne and myself.'

'My poor nymph, in such proper company what could Mr Alleyne possibly fear? Cheer up, brat. I think you may safely go to Vauxhall and enjoy the sights. If my dinner engagement is very boring, I may even look in myself, just to see how you go on!'

*   *   *

Despite Mr Alleyne's reservations, the journey to Vauxhall was unremarkable. There was a lengthy delay in crossing Westminster Bridge, which was the only route to the gardens. It was early in the season for the gardens, and the lamps had already been lit and twinkled gaily in a colourful display along the paths. Colonel Brentwood had secured a supper-box for them near the orchestra, and from there they watched the crowds while nibbling sweet biscuits washed down by glasses of Arrack punch. Lady Bilderston might have looked askance at the meagre portions provided, but Eustacia was too entranced by the colourful costumes and lively music to criticize the refreshments. The crowds pushed past the box in a noisy stream of rainbow colours, the masks adding a *frisson* of excitement to the atmosphere. Miss Pensford sat very quietly opposite Eustacia and eyed with disfavour the

119

jostling crowds. Lady Bilderston leaned forward to tap Mr Alleyne's sleeve with her fan.

'Perhaps, sir, you would like to take the girls to the north side of the gardens in readiness for the unveiling of the Cascade? It is nearly nine o'clock, and the Cascade is only displayed for fifteen minutes. Lady Trentham tells me that this year the illuminated landscape is very lifelike.'

'Oh, yes—yes, of course.'

Lady Bilderston turned to her elderly escort.

'You won't mind if we stay here and listen to the orchestra, Colonel?' Lady Bilderston shouted into his ear trumpet. 'These young people love the thrill of such spectacles, but you and I, sir, much prefer to avoid the throng, do we not?'

Colonel Brentwood nodded and beamed at her, and signalled to the waiter for more wine as Lady Bilderston watched Mr Alleyne walk away, a young lady on each arm.

*   *   *

Miss Marchant found the noise and bustle exhilarating, and looked about her in wide-eyed wonder. Miss Pensford, by contrast, clung to her escort, tense with apprehension. Mr Alleyne patted her hand and smiled down at her reassuringly.

'There is no need to be alarmed, Miss

Pensford. It is a little noisy, I know, but you are perfectly safe.'

She gave him a tremulous smile. 'Oh, I am not afraid, sir, not while you are with me.'

Miss Marchant tugged at his sleeve. 'Oh, Rupert—I have glimpsed the most fascinating little temple at the end of that walk—do say that we can go and explore, after we have seen the Cascade!'

As she spoke, a gentleman in a blue domino stopped, his head turned towards the little party. Miss Marchant, however, wrapped in a dove-grey domino and feeling secure behind her silk mask, noticed nothing, and continued to chatter away to her companions.

A bell rang out across the gardens, signalling that the Cascade was about to be uncovered, and the crowds began to push forward more quickly along the paths towards this spectacle. Caught in the throng, it was impossible for Mr Alleyne and his charges to walk together. Miss Pensford was still clinging to Rupert's arm, but the crowds held no terror for Eustacia, who happily fell behind. A small disturbance in one of the side alleys caught her attention and by the time she looked around again her companions had been swallowed up in the crowd. Miss Marchant was not unduly alarmed, knowing that everyone was moving in the direction of the Cascade. She would make her own way there, and if she did not come upon Rupert and Helen, it would not matter, for she was confident she could find her way back to her box. As she moved slowly along, she found a figure in a blue domino at her side.

'You appear to have no escort, Miss Marchant. Pray allow me to assist you.'

She jumped.

'Mr MacCauley! Thank you, but I assure you there is no need; my friends are only a little way ahead.'

'My dear ma'am, I cannot allow you to walk unattended.'

Eustacia hesitated. The press of people in the narrow path made it impossible for her to walk away from the gentleman, and she had to admit that his behaviour as he walked beside her was unexceptional: he took care to point out to her the delightful little grottoes and statues illuminated at each side of the path, and his knowledge of the gardens was sufficient for him to answer all her questions. When they reached the famed Cascade, the curtains before this extravaganza were just being drawn back, and a loud gasp of delight swelled from the crowd. Eustacia had to peer over the shoulders of those in front of her, but she thought the view worth the effort.

The scene before her was cunningly illuminated to represent a country landscape; in the foreground was a miller's house and glistening metal had been wrought to represent a waterfall that flowed down to turn the mill-wheel. At the foot of the scene, and visible only when Eustacia stood on tiptoe to see it, there was an illusion of foaming torrents of water pouring away out of sight. Eustacia joined in with the cries of delight, and when at last the curtains fell once more she turned away, her lips parted in a smile and her eyes twinkling through the slits of her mask.

'That was splendid! I am so glad I did not miss it!' she exclaimed.

Mr MacCauley chuckled beside her.

'I am delighted you enjoyed it. Now pray allow me to return you to your box.'

'Oh, but my friends are here, amongst the crowd. I am sure I can find them—'

'No, no, let me assure you that it would be quite impossible to find anyone in this crush,' replied her companion, taking her arm. 'Come, you will be quite safe with me.' The crowd was pushing back along the path, and Eustacia was content to move with it, her head still full of the scene she had just witnessed. When Mr MacCauley suggested they should take a short cut back to the Quadrangle she did not demur, but soon discovered that the route was much less well lit than the main path, and very soon they had left the crowd behind. Miss Marchant stopped.

'I think, sir, I would rather we returned to the main walk.' The gentleman smiled, and she felt him place one hand on her back.

'But this route will be much quicker, and

there is a series of little temples and grottoes to be seen on the way.'

'Thank you, but I—' She turned, but Mr MacCauley was standing very close and she found herself mask to mask with him. Only his mouth and chin were visible, but Eustacia thought his smile particularly wolf-like and predatory.

'My dear, may I tell you how enchanting you look in that mask?'

Miss Marchant fought off a momentary panic.

'Th-thank you, sir, but I fear all this excitement has been too much for me, or perhaps it was the plate of ratafia creams; it was rather foolish of me to eat all of them.'

The smile wavered. 'I beg your pardon?'

'Sir, I fear I am about to be most unwell,' she uttered in a strangled voice. She noticed that his smile had disappeared completely, and continued, 'It may of course have been the salmon; I was never partial to dill sauce. And then there was the syllabub.' Eustacia pressed one hand to her mouth and gave a hiccup. 'I am very sorry, sir, but please leave me—I would not have you watch as I disgrace myself!' She ran to one side of the path and leaned against a convenient tree trunk.

Mr MacCauley stared at her. 'Miss Marchant—'

'Please sir, just go!' she exclaimed, the words ending in a gasp as she shuddered dramatically and clung to the tree. Mr MacCauley hesitated. 'If you are sure . . .'

'Yes, yes, *go*!'

With a small bow, he turned and hurried away. Eustacia, watching him from the corner of her eyes, heaved a sigh of relief.

'Bravo, my dear.'

She jumped, peering into the darkness of the bushes where a black shape detached itself from the shadows.

'Vivyan! How long have you been there?'

'Long enough to appreciate your performance, brat. You should be on the stage! I presume you are not really feeling ill?'

'Oh, no,' came the cheerful reply. 'I could think of no other way of repulsing him.'

'Very true, but you really should not be wandering through the gardens alone, you know.'

'I do know it, but I became separated from Helen and Rupert, and then Nathan MacCauley appeared and—and I could not really get away from him without missing the Cascade.'

'Yes, I saw that, but you could have refused his escort afterwards.'

She gave an indignant gasp. 'You *saw* it? You watched him accompany me to the spectacle and did not come forward? You must know I would much rather have had your escort than that man!'

He bowed. 'Thank you, ma'am. I am

flattered.'

'Well, almost anyone would have been more acceptable!' She laughed. 'You must have realized I did not want his escort, why did you not make yourself known?'

'I did not want to be recognized. But you may be sure that I was keeping an eye on you.'

She made a mocking curtsy. 'La, I am grateful, sir!'

He grinned, and took her arm. 'Enough, brat. Come, I shall escort you back to your godmother.'

'And I suppose Rupert will consider that I am in a scrape again.' She sighed.

But when they arrived at Lady Bilderston's box, they found Mr Alleyne blaming himself for not providing a proper escort. Mr Lagallan interrupted him, saying with a faint smile, 'I have always found it impossible to give my attention to two ladies at one time.'

Mr Alleyne flushed, but before he could speak Miss Pensford broke in, saying, 'I have never liked crowds, and the press of people, all shouting and pushing, was far too daunting. I do not know what I would have done without Mr Alleyne's arm to support me.'

Lady Bilderston beamed at Vivyan.

'Well, thank you for returning my god-daughter to me, sir. Now you are here, Mr Lagallan, perhaps you would care to join us for supper?'

With a graceful bow, Vivyan accepted

her invitation.

'How delightful that you could join us after all, sir,' remarked Miss Pensford, inviting him to sit beside her.

'I only wish I could have joined you earlier and given you my escort,' he replied, smiling blandly at Eustacia, who had just choked on her wine.

'There are certainly some very ill-bred people amongst the crowds,' returned Miss Pensford, 'but I was never anxious for myself, I assure you.' She smiled warmly at Mr Alleyne, whose fair cheek reddened slightly.

'I am sorry I lost you in the crowd, Stacey,' he murmured, as Miss Pensford engaged Mr Lagallan in conversation. 'One moment you were beside me, then Helen—I mean Miss Pensford—was so alarmed by the jostling—'

'It does not matter, Rupert. I am very well able to take care of myself.'

The flush on his cheek darkened.

'You are angry with me. I have apologized, Eustacia; I don't see what else I could do. Surely you did not expect me to abandon Miss Pensford?'

'No, of course you could not do that,' Eustacia replied, wearily. 'Let us say no more of it. No harm has been done, and I did enjoy the Cascade! Let us also enjoy the supper that Godmama has so kindly provided for us.'

She turned her attention to the refreshments laid out before them. Lady

Bilderston might look dubiously at the wafer-thin slices of ham and chicken, and wonder if there was sufficient to satisfy the appetites of six persons, but Eustacia, having enjoyed a hearty dinner a few hours earlier, happily partook of the custards and cheesecakes, thanking her godmother profusely for such a splendid treat.

'Are you sure you should be eating so much, in view of your recent malaise?' murmured Vivyan, handing her a glass of punch.

Eustacia chuckled. 'I only hope Mr MacCauley does not observe me!'

'Oh? I thought you detested the man!'

'Well, and so I do, but I do not wish him to know that I duped him!'

Vivyan laughed at her, and shook his head, before his hostess claimed his attention.

*   *   *

Lady Bilderston had ordered her coach for midnight, well aware that the behaviour within the gardens could deteriorate alarmingly as the night wore on. Mr Lagallan's presence made it possible for each of the ladies to have their own escort out of the gardens, and at the gate the party broke up, with Vivyan inviting Mr Alleyne to accompany him to his club to finish off the night with a few games of chance. Rupert hesitated, but Lady Bilderston nodded benignly at him.

128

'Yes, do go, Mr Alleyne. You may be certain that with my footman up on the box, and Colonel Brentwood to attend us, we will be perfectly safe.'

Thus reassured, the young man climbed into Mr Lagallan's carriage for the journey back to town. Mr Alleyne was a little in awe of Vivyan, envying the older man his poise and knowledge of town life. However, nothing could have exceeded Mr Lagallan's friendliness that evening. He soon put Mr Alleyne at his ease, introduced him to his circle of friends at Brooks's, and looked after him so well that when they eventually left the club just as the first grey streaks of dawn were visible in the sky, that young gentlemen felt obliged to express his gratitude.

'I have not enjoyed an evening in Town so much, sir!' he said, pumping Mr Lagallan's hand vigorously.

'Yes, yes, thank you,' said Vivyan, pushing the young man into his coach. 'Allow me to drive you home.'

Mr Alleyne fell back against the squabs with an ecstatic sigh.

'Most wonderful evening,' he declared, his cheeks flushed from the quantities of wine he had imbibed.

Mr Lagallan watched him, a slight smile on his lips. 'Enjoyed Vauxhall, did you?'

'Oh, indeed! Vastly entertainin'!'

'But one has to be vigilant,' remarked

Vivyan. 'It is not the place for a lady to go unattended.'

'You are thinking of Stacey, I mean, Miss Marchant.' Rupert looked uncomfortable. 'I should not have allowed her to fall behind, but what could I do? Miss Pensford needed my arm, the path was too narrow for us all.'

'Of course.'

Mr Alleyne flushed. 'I know she is—that you are—what I mean is, Stacey told me that you and Miss Pensford are as good as engaged,' he confided, 'so you must know how much she dislikes crowds, and she is such a sweet, shy creature—'

'And Miss Marchant is much better able to look after herself?'

'Yes, that is it!' declared Rupert, gratified at his host's understanding. 'Stacey is a—a most redoubtable girl!'

'Well, I am happy that you think so, since I understand that you and she are to be married.'

There was a long silence, broken only by the clatter of the carriage as it rattled over the cobbles.

'Yes,' said Rupert at last. 'I suppose you heard that from your sister-in-law. I know she and Stacey are very close, must be, since Mrs Lagallan brought Stacey to London.' He peered across at his companion, who appeared as a shadowy figure in the darkened carriage. 'I suppose you know the full story?'

130

'I believe you met Miss Marchant in Somerset, where she lost her heart to you. Would you think me very forward if I said that you don't seem very happy with your engagement?'

Mr Alleyne bit his lip, but the camaraderie of the evening and the wine he had drunk overcame his natural reserve and he blurted out: 'No, damn it, I'm not! Oh, Stacey is a fine girl, and I admit that in Somerset I did perhaps pay her a little too much attention, but how was I to know she would follow me to London?'

'How indeed? Your father, I understand, does not approve of the marriage?'

'Well, I don't know about that. I only said that to Stacey so she would not think I was deserting her for no reason. I didn't want to hurt her, you see.'

In the darkness, Mr Lagallan's hands clenched into two purposeful fists, but he forced himself to stay calm.

'So would it not be better to make a clean breast of it now, and tell her the truth?'

'How can I?' cried Mr Alleyne, shrugging. 'She has come all this way to find me! It would break her heart if I were to draw back. Besides, it is not such a bad match; there is nothing my father could object to.'

'But you don't love her.'

'*Love!* No, I . . .'

The carriage had come to a halt, and Mr

Alleyne realized they had arrived at his lodgings. He thanked Mr Lagallan again for his hospitality, and climbed unsteadily out on to the flagway. As the coach pulled away, Mr Lagallan stared out of the window at the deserted streets, then with sudden violence he slammed his fist into the leather squabs.

CHAPTER TEN

The spell of fine weather continued, and Lady Bilderston could only marvel at Eustacia's energy. They might return from a rout or a masked ball in the early hours of the morning, but as my lady was sipping at her morning chocolate she would be informed by her maid that Miss Marchant had been up for some time, had taken Snuffles for his customary walk, and was even now engaged in some useful employment such as practising her music or dabbling with her watercolours.

*   *   *

In the afternoons, Eustacia rode out or walked with some of her growing number of friends, returning with just enough time to change for dinner before accompanying her godmother to the theatre or yet more parties. Such a busy schedule gave Eustacia little time for reflection, and that was exactly what she wanted.

When she had left Somerset, Miss Marchant's ambition had been simple: to find Rupert and marry him. But after two months in London, she found matters were a little more complicated. Rupert had agreed that they should be married as soon as he had spoken in person to his father. Since the evening at Vauxhall, she had not seen Vivyan, and she had to admit that she missed him. She glimpsed him occasionally at balls or assemblies, escorting Miss Pensford, but although he might acknowledge her with a bow and a slight smile, he never approached her. Eustacia wondered if she had in some way offended him, but when she did have the opportunity to tax him with this, he merely laughed. They were at one of the fashionable balls which occupied the evenings of the *ton*, and the movement of a country dance had thrown them together momentarily. Knowing it might be her only chance, Eustacia asked him bluntly if he was avoiding her.

'Of course not. Why should I do so?'

She wrinkled her nose.

'Well, that I don't know, but—I never see you any more!'

He smiled at her.

'That is only to be expected,' he said gently. 'We both of us have obligations.'

There had been no time for more, but for

Eustacia the enjoyment of the evening was at an end. She felt as if a cloud had descended over her, dimming her happiness.

And then there was Nathan MacCauley.

After their meeting at Vauxhall, he had sent her a small bouquet of flowers and a card, expressing his hope that she was quite recovered. Lady Bilderston was naturally at a loss to understand the message, and since Eustacia could not give her the full story, her godmother was amused to think that she should have a secret admirer. Miss Marchant decided that her maid must accompany her on any future outings, and she was thankful she had taken this precaution, because it seemed that Mr MacCauley was always on hand whenever she left the house. He had taken to walking in the little park, and he was often to be found riding in Hyde Park at the fashionable hour, always with some excuse to come up to talk to her.

Remembering their first meeting, Eustacia knew she must be careful in her dealings with the man, but he could be a charming companion, ready to tell her of his days adventuring through France with Vivyan— something that Mr Lagallan was reluctant to do. Eustacia listened with rapt attention to his lively discourse, even laughing aloud at the more comical of their escapades. At such times she forgot her suspicions and began to look upon Nathan MacCauley as a friend.

Mrs Lagallan, observing her young friend walking with Mr MacCauley, determined to warn her of the danger of being too intimate with the gentleman, and uttered her caution when they next rode out together.

Eustacia turned an innocent gaze upon her companion.

'You think I am too free with Mr MacCauley?'

'I am in no position to judge that, my dear, I am merely concerned that the man is an adventurer.'

'No more so than Vivyan.'

'But Vivyan's wildness has been somewhat tamed by his responsibilities. He has his estates to run now. From what he has told me, Nathan MacCauley has no such ties.'

'He is not so fortunate, then, as Vivyan,' murmured Eustacia. She noticed Mrs Lagallan's look of alarm and laughed. 'You need not worry, Caroline, I am in no danger of encouraging Nathan MacCauley!'

With this, Caroline had to be content, but she voiced her worries to her brother-in-law at the first opportunity. They were in the morning-room at Bruton Street, where Caroline was arranging roses in a glass bowl.

'Poor Stacey, she has no gentleman to protect her,' she remarked.

'She has Rupert Alleyne. He could soon send MacCauley to the right about.'

'But you know MacCauley, Vivyan. Could

you not have a word with him?'

Mr Lagallan laughed, but there was no humour in his voice.

'MacCauley is already suspicious of my involvement with Stacey; I don't want to stir that up again. Besides, I have no right to protect her. Let Alleyne do it.'

But Miss Marchant did not discuss Nathan MacCauley with Rupert. In fact, she discussed very little with Mr Alleyne, for the sad truth was that Miss Marchant was no longer sure of her own heart. The stern, preoccupied young man she now saw bore little resemblance to the carefree Rupert Alleyne who had romanced her in Somerset. Then, she had been thrilled to listen to his whispered endearments as they danced together, and to exchange stolen kisses in a secluded garden, but here in London Mr Alleyne was so circumspect he was almost pompous. When she had set out for London, Eustacia had believed she would throw herself into Rupert's arms and tell him everything, but she now knew that was impossible. He was shocked to think that she had run away from home and travelled in the company of Caroline Lagallan: how much worse he would think her if he knew the truth, and there was no way she could explain to him about Nathan MacCauley's behaviour without revealing something of her true journey to Town.

She mulled over this problem whilst riding

in the park, and as she made her way back to Fanshawe Gardens she was so engrossed with her concerns that she did not notice Mr Alleyne on the flagway until he called to her. She looked up.

'Rupert! Are you coming to see me?'

'Yes, I was on my way to tell you that I have had word from my father: I wanted to discuss it with you.'

'I see.' She jumped nimbly down from the saddle and handed her reins to the waiting groom.

'Miss Marchant, Stacey! I—'

'Pray step inside with me, Rupert, and we will discuss it.' Eustacia gave him a rather strained smile and accompanied him into the house. 'I am glad you have come,' she said, drawing off her gloves and tossing them together with her hat on to a side table, and waving away Avebury, the butler, who was coming towards them. 'Come into the morning-room, Rupert.'

'If I may have a word, Miss—' began the butler.

'Not now, Avebury.' She gave him a distracted smile. 'Pray tell my lady that I have returned, if you wish, but please make sure that Mr Alleyne and I are not disturbed.'

Without waiting for a reply, she swept Rupert into the morning-room, firmly closing the door upon the servant. Rupert walked into the middle of the room, then turned to face

Miss Marchant.

'Stacey, my father has written to tell me he will not be returning to Town until the autumn.' He paused, twisting his fine York gloves between his fingers. 'The thing is, I told you we could not go ahead with our engagement until I had spoken to him.'

'I know, Rupert, and at first I was angry at that—but it was wrong of me to be so impatient. You see, I know now—'

Mr Alleyne, locked into his own dilemma, scarcely heard her. He said bluntly, 'Well, this cannot go on until the autumn. I have treated you abominably.'

'No, Rupert, it is my fault. It was wicked of me to follow you to London. I should not have put you in this situation!'

'But I will make it up to you, Stacey. My mind is made up; I do not deserve you, but—'

Miss Marchant ran forward and took his hands.

'Please, Rupert, listen to me before you say any more!'

He looked down at her, frowning at her unusually serious expression, but before Eustacia could speak again they were interrupted by a stern, autocratic voice from the doorway.

'So, miss—this is how you spend your time in London!'

CHAPTER ELEVEN

The two young people jumped apart and turned to look at the elderly gentleman standing in the doorway. Miss Marchant recovered first, saying joyfully, 'Grandpapa! I had no idea you were here!'

'So I see,' said Sir Jasper, his countenance relaxing slightly as he noted her evident pleasure in seeing him. He allowed her to help him to a chair.

'Pray, sir, sit down here and tell me what has brought you to London?'

'*You* have, blister it!' he declared, glaring at her from under his bushy grey brows. 'You were supposed to be staying with that fool of a governess near Bath, and the next moment I get Bella's letter telling me she's invited you to stay and asking me to send on your clothes! Well, of course I agreed to it—often thought Bella should have put herself out more for you—but how did you get here, lass, eh? Your governess could tell me nothing of that, save to say that you had set off alone! Your Aunt Jayne is prostrate, thinking you have abandoned your family, so as soon as the doctor told me I was fit to travel, I set off to see for myself just what sort of scrape you had fallen into.'

'No scrape at all, Grandpapa,' Eustacia said

soothingly, dropping to her knees in front of the old gentleman. She possessed herself of his hands and turned her expressive green eyes upon his face. 'Oh, Grandpapa, it is such a tale that I could not put it all in a letter to you, but really, there was no need for you to post all the way to Town; I am sure Lady Bilderston told you I was perfectly safe.'

'Bella is a soft-hearted old fool!' he exclaimed, disposing scathingly of Lady Bilderston. 'Safe? Ha! What is your godmother about, to leave you alone with this young man?'

'What? Oh, of course, I had forgotten about Rupert.' Eustacia sprang to her feet. 'Grandfather, this—this is Mr Rupert Alleyne. You will remember we met him at the assemblies in Burnett—at least, Aunt Jayne met him, but you were recovering from your last illness, sir, and did not attend. Mr Alleyne was staying with his uncle, Sir Tristam, at Burnett Lodge.'

'Eh? Alleyne, did you say?' Sir Jasper peered at the young man. 'Hmm, I know your uncle, of course, but that's no reason for you to be alone here with my granddaughter.'

'No, sir, but you see, I can explain—'

'Hush, Rupert, perhaps it would be best if you left us,' interposed Eustacia. Mr Alleyne looked stubborn.

'No, Stacey, I think I should—'

'What's going on here, will someone tell me?' demanded Sir Jasper, banging his cane

140

on the floor.

'Yes, Grandpapa, all in good time, but first Mr Alleyne is leaving.'

'Oh no I'm not!' declared that young man, with such force that both Miss Marchant and her grandfather stared at him. He ran his tongue over his dry lips. 'It is not right that you should deal with this on your own, Eustacia. Sir Jasper, it—it is very fortuitous that you have arrived, sir, for I—I want to marry your granddaughter!'

Two pairs of eyes were fixed upon him. Eustacia clasped her hands together and lifted them to her mouth.

'Oh, Rupert, no!'

Mr Alleyne nodded, his face very pale.

'Yes, Eustacia. I came here today to tell you that this shilly-shallying must end.' He turned back to Sir Jasper, standing before him with the air of a schoolboy determined upon confession.

'You should know, sir, that it is all my fault that Miss Marchant came to London. She set out to find me, unworthy as I am, because I had—had given her to believe that I loved her—which I do, of course!' he added quickly. 'I—I left Somerset in the belief that it would be better for us both if we parted, but Eustacia has shown such—such *devotion*, such unswerving loyalty, that—' He broke off, biting his lip. 'Sir Jasper, it—it is my dearest wish, and Miss Marchant's, that you allow us to be married at the earliest opportunity.'

Eustacia stared at Rupert, tears starting in her eyes.

'Oh, Rupert!' she whispered.

He gave her a strained smile.

'I know I should have spoken sooner, it was cowardly of me to put it off.'

Sir Jasper tapped his cane again.

'Are you telling me that this—this *liaison* started in Burnett?'

'Grandpapa—'

'Yes, sir. I behaved reprehensibly towards Miss Marchant. I should have called upon you then, but I thought—I thought it too soon, that our affection would not last.'

'Grandfather, I think we should talk,' said Eustacia, her face as pale as her kerchief.

'Plenty of time for that later,' declared the old man, waving away her arm as he pushed himself out of his seat. 'Alleyne—I remember you now: I knew your father, too, many years ago. Fine man.'

'Thank you, sir.'

'He had several estates, I believe. Are they still in the family?' He shot a fierce glance at Mr Alleyne, who nodded.

'Yes, sir. We have properties in Berkshire and Dorset, as well as the hunting-lodge in Leicestershire, and of course the estate in Yorkshire . . .'

'Splendid, splendid. And you are his eldest son?'

'His only son, Sir Jasper.'

'Excellent! Well, well, I think we can clear up this business now, if the two of you are so set upon the match. If my Stacey came all the way to London to find you, sir, she must be serious about you! Well then, Mr Alleyne, give me your hand! You have my blessing.'

Somewhat bemused, Mr Alleyne took the proffered hand. Eustacia gave a little whimper.

'Well, well,' exclaimed Sir Jasper, smiling now, 'a fine day's work! I will compose a notice for the *Gazette,* and—'

'*No!*' Eustacia's cry brought her grandfather's eyes upon her. Flushing, she said more quietly, 'Grandpapa, I—I think we must wait until Rupert has had time to discuss this with his father. I—I would not want him to think we are in unseemly haste to wed.'

'Hmm, I suppose you are right,' agreed Sir Jasper. He smiled at his granddaughter. 'Now, I expect you are wishing me elsewhere, eh, puss? Very well, I shall go and find your godmama, and give her the good news!' He nodded towards Mr Alleyne. 'I'll give you ten minutes alone with my granddaughter, but no more, or we shall have all the tongues a-wagging!' Then, chuckling to himself, Sir Jasper walked slowly out of the room.

Eustacia gazed across the room at Mr Alleyne.

'Well,' said the young man eventually, 'there it is. We are engaged.'

'Yes,' agreed Eustacia, in a hollow voice.

'I did not think it would be so easy,' he confessed. 'I—I think my father might be a little harder to persuade.'

'Yes.'

Rupert looked at her, his eyes narrowed.

'Stacey—what is it, are you ill? This is what you wanted, is it not?'

Pulling herself out of her reverie, Eustacia summoned up a bright smile.

'But of course! I came all the way to London just for this moment!'

Mr Alleyne took her hand.

'Good,' he said. 'I'm glad I've made you happy.' Gently he kissed her lips, then drew back, flushing and laughing. 'Sorry—I mean— I must go!'

With another half-smile he left the room, and for several minutes Eustacia did not move, merely stared at the door then, with a sob, she fled to the seclusion of her bedchamber.

*   *   *

It could not be expected that such news would remain a secret. Lady Bilderston made only her closest friends privy to the engagement, and in the strictest confidence, so that by the time Eustacia arrived at Almack's a few days later, everyone was congratulating her. Even Miss Pensford, in her cool way, told her how fortunate she was.

'Mr Alleyne is the most charming young man in London, Eustacia. I hope you will make him happy.'

'At least as happy as you will make Vivyan!' retorted Miss Marchant. She was immediately sorry for her outburst, but Miss Pensford was in no way discomposed.

'There is a difference in our circumstances,' came the cool reply. 'Yours is very much a love-match, whereas Mr Lagallan and I are marrying for far more practical considerations, therefore there is no reason why our union should *not* be a success.' Eustacia stared at her.

'Do you feel nothing for him, then? Surely you must agree he is the most handsome gentleman in Town?'

'To be truthful, no,' replied Helen. She added, not meeting her friend's eyes, 'I—I do not find dark men attractive.'

Unable to think of a suitable reply that would not seriously jeopardize their friendship, Miss Marchant left her, but their conversation came to mind again when Vivyan approached Stacey later that evening.

'I have come to beg a dance with you, while I still may,' he announced, his dark eyes glinting.

'You have heard, then.' She tried to smile, but was uncertain of its success.

'Yes. Caroline told me. She had it from Lady Trentham this morning. Congratulations.'

'Thank you.' She stole a glance up at him. 'You sound a little . . . angry.'

'Do I? My apologies. I am perhaps a little disappointed that you did not tell me yourself.'

'It—it was meant to be a secret. My grandfather arrived in town three days ago, and Rupert immediately approached him, but it was agreed that nothing should be announced until Rupert has had the opportunity to talk to his father.'

'I see. And where is the fortunate bridegroom tonight?'

'He is here, somewhere.' She looked about her. 'Yes, over there—in fact, he is dancing with Helen.' For a moment she watched them; they were laughing, their fair heads almost touching. Mr Lagallan voiced her thoughts.

'They make a handsome couple.'

'Yes. Yes, they do.'

He did not miss the wistful note in her voice, and glanced down at her.

'What ails you, brat?'

She sighed. 'I fear I have enjoyed a surfeit of parties. I feel . . . stifled, somehow.' She gave him a brief smile. 'Is it not ironic that now I have achieved everything I worked for, I should want something different? If I was in the country, I should go for a long ride, and gallop away these crotchets.'

'You can ride in the park.'

'Yes, at a very ladylike pace!' She laughed at him as they separated for the movement of

146

the dance.

When they came back together, Vivyan said: 'I think I have the answer! We should have an outing, the four of us, to celebrate our forthcoming nuptials. A ride and a picnic! There is some very fine countryside around Hampstead, where we can enjoy a gallop. A friend of mine owns a property with a pretty little park near Driver's Hill, a few miles north of Hampstead, and I am sure he will allow us to picnic there. A note to him tomorrow would secure permission. What do you say?'

Eustacia's stammered reply was lost as they separated once more, but he did not need to hear it, reading her answer in the eloquent look she bestowed upon him.

For the remainder of the dance Eustacia set her mind to arrangements for the planned treat. As soon as the music stopped, she dragged Mr Lagallan off the floor to put the idea to Helen and Rupert.

'The town is growing so hot!' she declared. 'I long to ride out into the country!' She looked up at Vivyan. 'Do you think that Caroline would agree to come along, to act as chaperone? I am sure Godmama, and my grandfather too, will feel obliged to accompany us in the carriage if she does not.'

Faced with such enthusiasm, the others agreed to the scheme, and Vivyan promised to make the necessary arrangements and ask his sister-in-law to accompany them.

The timing was fortuitous. The good weather held, and on a sunny morning Miss Pensford and Mr Alleyne rode into Fanshawe Gardens to meet Eustacia. The carriages carrying the picnic had gone on ahead, and once Eustacia was mounted upon her long-tailed grey, all that was left to do was to await the arrival of Mr Lagallan and his sister-in-law. A few moments later, three riders were seen approaching.

'Here are Caroline and Vivyan now—and the Major is with them!' Miss Marchant held out her hand to him, smiling. 'Well, sir, we are honoured that you should join us!'

He grasped her fingers briefly and smiled at her.

'I thought I might come along and help Caroline contain your high spirits.' He cast an appreciative eye over her mount. 'She looks a lively little mare, but you seem to have the measure of her. I look forward to seeing her in action once we reach open country.'

'You shall, sir! I own that I too want to try the mare's paces. So far I have only been able to canter in the park!'

At last the little party set off, keeping a sedate pace. Once Oxford Street had been negotiated, they kept to the quieter side streets and lanes as far as Tottenham Court crossroads. Vivyan and Major Lagallan led the way, with Mr Alleyne riding alongside Miss Pensford, while Caroline and Eustacia followed with Lady Bilderston's groom riding at a discreet distance behind them. Eustacia kept up a constant flow of lively chatter, but Mrs Lagallan observed how often her eyes strayed to Rupert Alleyne.

'Miss Pensford appears to be a nervous rider. I think Mr Alleyne is concerned for her.'

Eustacia glanced at her companion.

'I beg your pardon? Oh, yes—yes. Rupert is the most considerate of men. Did you think I might be jealous? I have known Helen for so many years, I have no fear that she will flirt with Rupert.'

Mrs Lagallan tried unsuccessfully to stifle a sigh. 'Yes, she has every virtue.'

Eustacia bit her lip. 'Caroline—forgive me if I am impertinent, but—Vivyan does not love Helen, does he? So why is he going to marry her?'

'He says it is time he settled down.'

'But she will make him miserable!' cried Eustacia, before she could stop herself.

'I think you might be right,' agreed Caroline, 'but now he has offered for her, he will not go back on it. We must hope that we are wrong. After all, many men are perfectly happy in such marriages.'

'But not Vivyan! He has too much spirit, he is so—so *alive*!' Caroline smiled.

'I said very much the same thing about him, many years ago, when he was a boy. But he is not a child now, Stacey. He has made his choice.'

As they left Tottenham behind them and headed north on the Hampstead road, the two ladies moved up to join the other riders. Mr Lagallan raised his crop, pointing towards a stretch of open country to the right.

'Caro, are you ready to gallop the fidgets from your hack? And you, Stacey, shall we see what that little mare of yours can do? Philip and I are going to race to that copse up there on the hill.'

'By all means!' declared Eustacia, kicking her mare on. 'Come on, Bianca, show them your heels!'

Scenting a race, the horses leapt forward. Major Lagallan was soon leading the way on his big hunter, with Vivyan in hot pursuit. Eustacia gave herself up to the excitement of the chase. She was aware of horses pounding behind her, but she did not look round, revelling in the wind on her skin and the thunder of hoofs as they flew across the turf. All too soon it was over. They reached the copse and the horses slowed. Eustacia brought her mare up alongside Vivyan's rangy black stallion.

'Well, Stacey, better now?' He grinned at her.

She laughed up at him, her eyes shining.

'That was wonderful! Bianca has the most beautiful action! I have never ridden her so hard before, and we were gaining on you!' She added mischievously, 'Another few lengths and we would have been neck and neck!'

'Ha! You flatter yourself, brat. I wasn't even trying!'

Their banter was interrupted by Mr Alleyne, who rode up at that moment, his eyes positively blazing.

'Just what do you think you are about?' he demanded furiously.

Mr Lagallan looked at him, his brows raised. 'I beg your pardon?'

'When you all set off like that, it was obvious that the other horses would want to follow! Miss Pensford could not hold back her mount, and she has had the most wretched time of it! I assure you she did not wish to go careering across the country like a hoyden at breakneck speed!'

'Do you imply that is what I was doing, Rupert?' demanded Miss Marchant, her eyes glittering dangerously.

'You know very well it is different for you, Stacey. You are a natural horsewoman, but Miss Pensford might well have been thrown!'

Eustacia looked around: Miss Pensford did indeed appear to be flustered. Her usually neat hair had worked its way loose from her bonnet, and little tendrils were curling about her face. She looked very cross. Miss Marchant

151

immediately wheeled about, saying as she rode up to her, 'Oh, Helen, I am so sorry. I did not think! But we have been riding together before, at home, and you were never worried by it.'

'At home I have my own dear Snowball to ride. This hired hack is very different. Once he had made up his mind, there was no stopping him; I could only hold on and hope I would not be tossed out of my seat.' Miss Pensford managed a little smile. 'Just give me a little more notice before you race off again, that I may call the groom to help me control this beast.'

Having assured herself that Helen was happy to continue, Eustacia turned away, her high spirits flattened. Mr Alleyne drew alongside her.

'I do not know how you came to be so thoughtless!' he muttered, in a furious undervoice.

'I think the blame rests with Caroline and myself,' remarked Major Lagallan, turning his charming smile upon Miss Pensford. 'We were invited along to keep you young people in order, and we have behaved like veritable children ourselves, for the temptation to race was just too strong. My apologies, Miss Pensford. I trust you are not hurt?'

Succumbing to the coaxing tone, Miss Pensford smiled, somewhat mollified.

'Thank you, Major, I am not hurt. I am

sorry to have caused so much concern. My horse would not be stopped, but there was never any real danger, the groom was very close, and Mr Alleyne matched my pace all the way, so I was not abandoned.' She threw that young man a grateful smile.

Major Lagallan nodded. 'Very well, then. Shall we continue?'

As they moved off, Eustacia glanced towards Mr Alleyne, but he ignored her. She realized he was still very angry.

'Don't worry, brat, he'll come about.'

She turned to find Vivyan beside her.

'Rupert is right; it *was* thoughtless of me. I had not considered that Helen might not wish to race.'

'She came to no harm.' His dark eyes glinted. 'Miss Pensford is not the sort to need rescuing from scrapes.'

Eustacia had a sudden, vivid memory of her first meeting with Vivyan; tears pricked her eyelids.

'Stacey—what is it?'

His concern was unbearable. Muttering an excuse she turned away from him, urging her mare into a trot until she had caught up with Caroline Lagallan, and she rode beside her until they reached the gates of Kenton Park.

'Our host has a prior engagement and sends his apologies that he cannot greet us in person,' explained Vivyan. 'He was also good enough to say that if the weather should turn inclement, we may repair to the house for shelter.'

Fortunately, they had no need to resort to such measures. The meal, served alfresco in the shade of a towering chestnut tree, did much to restore the party's spirits, although Mr Alleyne was still angry with Eustacia, and this manifested itself in his studious attentions towards Miss Pensford.

Sitting beside Mrs Lagallan, Eustacia surreptitiously watched Rupert as he escorted Miss Pensford to a shady seat, selected the most succulent dishes to tempt her appetite and hovered around her, as solicitous as any courtier. She was a little afraid that Vivyan might take exception to such behaviour, but a look reassured her that Mr Lagallan was deep in conversation with his brother, discussing the latest peace negotiations.

When their meal was finished, Major Lagallan took his wife off for a stroll, and Vivyan threw himself down on the rug beside Miss Marchant.

'Well, nymph, are you pleased with your little outing?'

Eustacia smiled; the fine wine provided by the major had made her sleepy and content.

'Extremely,' she murmured. 'We should picnic at least once a month when we are in Town.'

'But this time next year we shall both be married, and most likely buried on our estates,' Vivyan reminded her. 'I think Helen will want to play the great lady to her neighbours.'

Eustacia gave her attention to picking daisies from the short grass.

'And you will be there with her, Vivyan?'

'Of course. I shall be the model husband.'

'Will you?' She turned her direct gaze upon him. 'Will that make you happy, Vivyan?'

A black frown darkened his brow. He sat up. 'Don't, Stacey.'

'I want you both to be happy, Vivyan.'

'I shall give Helen no cause for complaint.'

Eustacia gave a little smile.

'That is not quite the same thing,' she said. 'You don't love her, do you?'

'I have offered for her, and she has accepted me. I cannot go back on it. Gentlemen don't cry off from an engagement.' A wry smile twisted his mouth. 'You are still young enough to follow your dreams, Stacey. I pray they will come true for you.' He jumped to his feet. 'The wind is getting up. We had best be heading back.'

*   *   *

The riders decided to skirt the bustling spa town of Hampstead on their return journey, Vivyan leading them unerringly through the labyrinth of country lanes to rejoin the main road just north of Tottenham.

'Vivyan, I am always amazed at your powers of navigation,' declared Caroline, as they trotted out on to the wider road and waited for the rest of the group to catch up.

'One of the few benefits of my wild youth, Caro! I spent many a night at that inn we passed at Frith.'

Caroline nodded at Miss Marchant, who was riding beside her. 'We thought as much when we noticed how the landlord doffed his cap to you!'

Vivyan grinned. 'Aye, old Reedman was always ready to turn a blind eye to our sprees. For a fee, of course. And it's well known that The Sun is the haunt for more than one gentleman of the road.'

'Do you mean highwaymen?' breathed Eustacia. 'You've *met* them?'

'Well, they weren't introduced to me as such!'

'Pray, Stacey, don't encourage him,' begged Caroline, her eyes twinkling. 'Vivyan has left that world behind him now, have you not, brother?'

'To be sure I have, but it is always useful to know such a landlord. One never knows when it might be necessary.'

Mrs Lagallan frowned at him but said no more, for Miss Pensford and Mr Alleyne had joined them, and she quickly turned the conversation to more unexceptional topics. Miss Marchant became lost in thought as they rode back into town, and did not notice how far she had dropped behind the others until Caroline turned her horse to wait for her.

'Poor Stacey, are you so very tired?'

'Not a bit of it!' Eustacia replied, smiling. 'I was merely daydreaming.'

'By the by, I must write to Lady Bilderston. We are going out of town next week, and will not be able to attend her party.'

'Oh, and—and will you be away long?'

'I am taking the children to Worthing. Philip has business in Town, so Vivyan has offered to take us. He is going to stay for a few days to help us settle in. His carriage is so well sprung, and little Philip is such a bad traveller, I hope it will be better for him. Pray don't look so downhearted, my love.'

'I cannot help it! Godmama has arranged the party on Wednesday especially for me, and I did so want you to be there. And I was hoping you would be at Lady Addingham's dress ball on the Saturday. Godmama says it will be the most spectacular of the season, and she has bought me yet another new gown, and—oh, I shall miss you, Caroline!'

Mrs Lagallan leaned across and patted her hand.

'And I shall miss you, my love, but I have no doubt that we shall meet again in Town this winter! Besides, Vivyan has promised to attend the Addingham party—he is travelling back on Saturday morning so that he will not miss it.

You may show off your new gown to him—I know you value his opinion above anything I could tell you! Now, let us enjoy a little gallop and catch up with the others.'

*   *   *

Over the next few days, it seemed to Eustacia that many of her friends were planning to leave London. As Town grew hotter, families began to talk of removing to the coast or returning to their country retreats. Never a lover of town life, Sir Jasper was eager to return to Somerset and suggested that Eustacia should come back with him until such time as Mr Alleyne could discuss their engagement with his elusive parent.

'Young Alleyne can come, too, if that would make you happy,' Sir Jasper added, seeing her look of dismay. But in the end it was agreed that he would leave Eustacia with her godmother until Lady Bilderston herself removed to Brighton at the beginning of July.

'Well, that works out splendidly!' Sir Jasper told Mr Alleyne, who had joined them at Fanshawe Gardens for Sir Jasper's last dinner in Town. 'Your father is due in London at the end of June, is he not? I shall leave a letter for him, my boy, and trust we shall be able to secure this engagement and announce it before Bella here leaves Town.'

Miss Marchant did not think Mr Alleyne

looked at all delighted with this news, and when they gathered in the drawing-room later that evening she waited until Lady Bilderston and her grandfather were engrossed in a game of backgammon before drawing Rupert away to the window, ostensibly to show him her latest watercolour. She drew a deep breath.

'Rupert, perhaps—perhaps we should not go ahead with this engagement.'

He stared at her. 'What are you saying, Stacey?'

'I—that is—Rupert, I am not sure that we should—'

He caught her hands. 'My dear, you are still upset because I was angry with you over that foolish ride!'

'No, no—but . . . I do not want us to make a mistake.'

'Silly puss, how can that be?' he said, smiling down at her. 'You risked so much to find me! Was ever a man so undeserving of such fidelity?'

'Rupert, you are not undeserving! Indeed, you deserve far more than I can ever give you—'

'Now that is quite enough!' He frowned at her, laying one finger over her lips. 'Promise me you will say no more about it. We have your grandfather's blessing, and I am sure my father will not object. If all goes well, we could be married by Christmas.' He smiled suddenly.

'And I tell you what I shall do! There is a new play opening at Covent Garden—I shall secure a box, and escort you and your godmama to see it! There, that will be a high treat, will it not?'

'Yes, of course. That is very kind of you, Rupert, but—'

The entry of the tea tray interrupted their discussion, and there was no opportunity for any further private talk before Rupert took his leave shortly after eleven o'clock.

*   *   *

After waving goodbye to her grandfather the next morning, Miss Marchant hoped for a period of quiet reflection to help her unravel her tangled thoughts, but she had scarcely had time to sit down in the morning-room with Lady Bilderston, when Mr Alleyne was announced.

'Good news!' declared that young man, as soon as he had greeted his hostess. 'You will recall I told you last night that I would take you to see the new play at Covent Garden? Well, a good friend of mine has broken his leg—not that *that* is good news, of course, but he had taken a box at the theatre for this very evening, and now that he cannot go he has offered the tickets to me!' He smiled at the ladies. 'Well, what shall I tell him—are you free to attend tonight?'

Lady Bilderston beamed at his glowing countenance.

'How kind of you to think of us, dear boy! I admit I would dearly love to go with you—what do you say, Eustacia?'

'I should like to go,' agreed Miss Marchant, 'but are we not promised to attend Lady Oakham's rout this evening?'

Lady Bilderston shook her head. 'No, no, I thought we might look in there, but it was never firmly agreed, you know. Well, my dear?'

Eustacia hesitated, then smiled. 'Very well, let us go to the theatre!'

*   *   *

By the time Lady Bilderston's carriage clattered across the piazza, the theatre was already filling up. Mr Alleyne ushered his guests into the box, placing their chairs for the best view and behaving so attentively that, as they took their seats, Lady Bilderston could not help observing to Eustacia how fortunate she was in her choice of bridegroom. Miss Marchant gave her attention to the stage and did not reply, but she felt as if the net were closing ever tighter about her.

Rupert had arranged for refreshments to be served in the interval, and while he pointed out to Eustacia the little delicacies he had chosen for her, Lady Bilderston was free to seek out familiar faces in the auditorium, and she entertained them with a constant flow of chatter.

'Goodness, there is Mary Leavenham! Breeding again, I see. And Eliza Trentham— look, Stacey, she is waving! Pray acknowledge her, my dear, she is such a good friend!'

Obediently, Eustacia looked up to wave to Lady Trentham.

'Oh, look, Godmama! Over there. Is that not Viv—Mr Lagallan?'

'Why yes, child. I believe you are right. But who is that with him? Young Viscount Denny, I think, and several other young bucks.'

Eustacia waved energetically.

'He has seen us!' she declared, smiling, as Mr Lagallan raised his hand in salute. 'I wonder if he will come to our box?'

Rupert scowled. 'I hope he will not attempt it, for the performance is about to begin, and you will not wish to be interrupted. Come, Stacey, will you not try this marzipan? It is very good.'

*   *   *

Mr Lagallan did not interrupt them, but Stacey had little time to miss him: there were the delightful sweetmeats to be sampled, and the play to entertain her, so that when the little party left the theatre shortly after midnight Eustacia was more in charity with Mr Alleyne than she had been since her arrival in London.

162

'A truly splendid evening, Rupert. Thank you so much for arranging everything just so!'

With Miss Marchant's sparkling glance upon him, a delicate flush tinged Rupert's fair cheek. He muttered a disclaimer and, setting his hat firmly over his blond curls, he escorted the ladies out of the theatre.

Despite the hour, the piazza was full of voices, shouting to make themselves heard over the noise of the carriages which jostled for a space to pick up their patrons. Eustacia's head was still buzzing with the performance, and she could not be still. She walked away from the crowd at the theatre entrance, knowing that Lady Bilderston's coach would not be able to get near for some time yet. As she approached the corner of the building, she heard a sound; a human voice, she thought. Someone whimpering. Moving cautiously towards the shadowy side alley, Eustacia tried to blot out the noise of the crowd behind her, and this time she distinctly heard a low moaning, then the sound of someone sobbing. She peered into the blackness.

'Who's there?' she called.

Silence greeted her. She tried again, stepping a little further into the alley.

'Please show yourself, I want to help you.'

After a long moment, a figure detached itself from the shadows and moved slowly towards her. Eustacia saw it was a young girl, holding a worn red cloak about her shoulders.

Dusky curls escaped around the edges of her mob cap, and as the girl lifted her head Eustacia caught her breath at the swollen lip and ugly bruising that disfigured her face.

'Oh, you poor child!' exclaimed Eustacia, with ready sympathy. 'What has happened to you?'

She reached for the girl, guiding her out of the darkness with one arm around her trembling shoulders.

'Who did this to you?' she asked.

'A gen'leman.' The girl spoke with difficulty through her cracked and swollen lips. 'Acos' I wouldn't—I wouldn't—'

'No gentleman would do this!' muttered Miss Marchant. 'Come, my dear, tell me where you live. I shall take you home.'

Tears spilled over the bruised cheeks.

'I ain't got no 'ome. I—I ran away, see. Got a ride on a wagon into Lunnon.'

'Did you think to get work here?' Eustacia asked, her voice warm with sympathy.

The girl shook her head.

'I—I come to find Tom. 'E's my beau, see, and 'e come to Lunnon to be a footman in a lord's 'ouse. 'E said 'e would send fer me, but I couldn't wait. I 'ad to tell 'im, to tell 'im . . .'

'Tell him what, my dear?'

The girl burst into tears, sobbing loudly, and Eustacia drew her into her arms, her warm heart touched by such misery. By this time, Lady Bilderston had come in search of her god-daughter. At the sight of Miss Marchant with her arms about the decidedly shabby figure, my lady threw up her hands.

'Mercy me, what is this, Eustacia? What is amiss here?' she demanded, as she approached with Mr Alleyne beside her.

Eustacia's green eyes glittered angrily as she looked over the sobbing girl's head.

'This poor child has been attacked. I found her crying in the alleyway, and she tells me she does not live in London. We must take her with us, Godmama, and look after her until we can take her safely home again.'

Lady Bilderston drew back in horror.

'My dear child, you cannot take up a perfect stranger!'

'Well, neither can we leave her here,' reasoned Miss Marchant.

Mr Alleyne pulled out his purse.

'If you wish, I will give the girl the fare for a hack to take her home.'

'She *has* no home!' declared Miss Marchant. 'She—she ran away to London.'

A small crowd was beginning to gather, and Rupert looked about him uneasily.

'Stacey,' he hissed, 'look at her clothing. She is a serving-wench.'

'She is no less a child!' retorted Eustacia, her arms tightening around the shaking form.

'M-Miss Marchant, I beg you—leave her.' said Rupert. 'We are beginning to attract attention.'

Eustacia looked up, noticing for the first time the interested faces gathered about them. She was unconcerned with their curiosity, and soon returned her attention to the girl, who was still sobbing quietly.

*   *   *

At the edge of the crowd, a gentleman in a silk evening cloak lowered his quizzing-glass and flicked an amused glance at his companion.

'I can see no scarlet stockings, old friend, but would that be . . . ?'

Mr Lagallan's mouth twisted into a wry smile.

'Yes, Denny,' he murmured, 'it would!'

*   *   *

Eustacia fixed Lady Bilderston with an anxious gaze.

'Godmama, pray say we may take her up with us.'

'Well—that is—I— Oh, my child, how can you be sure she is telling the truth?'

'Quite so,' agreed Rupert, trying to take control. He held out his hand towards Miss Marchant. 'Come along now,' he said firmly. 'This is not your concern.'

'It is the concern of *every* Christian!' she flashed, her eyes very bright.

'If I might make a suggestion?' said a voice.

Eustacia looked round as Mr Lagallan stepped out of the crowd. He was smiling, but not unkindly. He bowed to Lady Bilderston.

'Ma'am, I believe I saw your carriage but a few yards away: perhaps Mr Alleyne should direct it here?' He watched as that young gentleman nodded eagerly and hurried off, then he turned back to the ladies. 'I think, my lady, it would do no harm to take the girl with you, if Miss Marchant is set upon it.' His lips twitched as he surveyed the crowd around them. 'You can then continue this discussion in—ah—a more private mode.'

Lady Bilderston pouted.

'I have to say I think you are right, sir.' She gave a sigh. 'Very well. Come, Stacey, bring the child.'

The carriage rumbled up to them, scattering the onlookers, and Rupert jumped down ready to hand in his charges. His jaw dropped when Eustacia approached, her arm still firmly about the girl's shoulders.

'Y-you cannot take her in the coach!'

'Well, I don't know what else we are going to do with her!' snapped Lady Bilderston, exasperated.

The smile in Mr Lagallan's eyes deepened.

'Denny and I will make room for you in my carriage, Alleyne, if you would prefer that,' he said softly.

Rupert's lips thinned. He said stiffly, 'Thank you, but I think I know my duty!'

Eustacia bundled the girl into the coach.

'Pray do not come with us if you are going to be horridly cross, Rupert!'

'He is not cross, my dear,' drawled Vivyan. 'He is merely concerned at the tongues that will wag over this!'

Miss Marchant's chin went up.

'Let them wag!'

In the far corner of the carriage, Lady Bilderston threw up her hands.

'My dear child, pray do not talk so! Mr Alleyne, do not stand there in the doorway— are you coming with us or not?'

'Of course he is.' Mr Lagallan gave Rupert a gentle push. 'Go to it, Alleyne. It's a rare thing in these modern times for a gentleman to have such an opportunity to rescue a damsel in distress!'

As Mr Alleyne climbed into the coach, muttering under his breath, Eustacia glanced out of the window at Vivyan, a slight doubt shadowing her eyes. Meeting her glance, he smiled, and Eustacia relaxed, insensibly cheered by his silent support.

The coach rattled through the dark streets, and Miss Marchant kept her arm about the young girl, thankful that the tears had now subsided to the occasional sob.

'Do you know,' she said, handing the child her own snowy handkerchief, 'I think we would go on more comfortably if we knew what to call you. What is your name, my dear?'

168

'N-Nan,' came the stumbling reply.

'Nan. What a pretty name. And you came to London to find your beau?'

'Yes'm.'

'Well, perhaps tomorrow I shall help you to find him.'

'Oh, no!' Nan turned two dark and tearful eyes towards Miss Marchant. 'No, ma'am, 'tis no use! I's already seen 'im, but 'e says—'e says . . .' She stopped, fighting back a fresh bout of tears. ' 'E says 'e can't 'elp me, bein' as 'ow 'e's new to 'is post.' She twisted the handkerchief between her fingers. 'T—Tom says 'e can't consider a wife until 'e's first footman, at least!' Tears ran down her bruised cheeks. ' 'E don't want to marry me, miss! I d-don't think 'e ever thought of marryin' me!'

'Oh, my poor child! Did Tom do this to you?' Miss Marchant gently brushed the dusky curls from the girl's wounded forehead.

'Oh, no, miss, that weren't Tom! After I see'd 'im this mornin', I thought p'raps I could find work, that mebbe Tom'd change 'is mind, when 'e'd 'ad chance to get used to me bein' around. B-but no one'd take me, 'cos I ain't got no letters tellin 'em that I's honest and 'ard workin'. Then Mrs Bates comes up to me, very kind, like, and she says I could stay with 'er, and she'd look after me, and if I was a good girl, and did as I was bid, I should 'ave a room of me own, and—and a good wage.' Eustacia felt a shudder run through the girl's body.

'She—she took me to 'er 'ouse, and put me in a room with . . . with a man. "There you are, sir," she says. "A ripe peach for 'ee, fresh from the country." And then she goes out . . . and—and locks the door.'

Lady Bilderston tutted, and Mr Alleyne shifted uncomfortably in his seat.

'Really, Eustacia, I think this should wait—'

'Nonsense, Rupert. It is better that the child finish her tale as soon as may be. Go on, Nan, pray do not be frightened.'

The girl shuddered again, and glanced up at the shadowy figures around her.

' 'E—'e kissed me,' she whispered. 'But it—it wasn't like Tom's kisses. These were hard, and—and—' She broke off, burying her head against Stacey's shoulder. 'I—I wanted 'im to stop, Miss, but 'e only laughed, and when I tried to push 'im away, that's when 'e belted me.'

Eustacia felt the tears welling in her own eyes, and she had to blink them away.

'Poor Nan,' she muttered. 'Don't worry, my dear, no one shall hurt you again, you have my word on it. Is that not right, Godmama?'

'Yes, yes, but how did the child come to be in the alley beside the theatre?'

'I—I escaped through a window.'

'Oh, good for you!' declared Miss Marchant. 'And no one came after you?'

Nan shook her head.

'There was an 'eavy candlestick on the table,

170

and I—I 'it the man with it. 'E fell to the floor. I don't *think* I killed 'im.'

'Little matter if you did,' muttered Eustacia. 'I think we should inform the magistrates!'

Rupert uttered a strangled cry.

'Stacey! Would you have us embroiled in *murder?*'

'I would have the villain pay for his crimes!' retorted Eustacia, fiercely. She looked down at the girl. 'Nan, dear, do you think you could find Mrs Bates's house again?'

But Nan merely shook her head, declaring that she had been walking for over an hour, and had no idea of her route.

'Well, I've no doubt this little episode has given you a distaste for the town,' remarked Rupert. 'If Lady Bilderston will be kind enough to give you a bed for the night, I will find you the fare to go home in the morning.'

'But I *can't* go 'ome, sir!' wailed Nan. 'I can't never go 'ome!'

'Hush, child, pray do not distress yourself,' said Miss Marchant, hugging her. 'Why do you say you cannot go home?'

The girl hiccuped.

'Acos',' she whispered, 'acos' I'm with child.'

CHAPTER TWELVE

At these words, Lady Bilderston sank back in her seat with a low moan, and Rupert was obliged to smother an oath. Only Eustacia seemed unaffected. She did indeed blink, but did not remove her arms from the girl's plump shoulders.

'Is it Tom's baby, Nan?' she asked, gently.

The girl nodded.

'And does he know?'

'Y—yes.'

'And still he will not marry you?'

' 'E—'e said 'tisn't 'is—'e said I'm a—a—but I *ain't!*' cried Nan. 'Believe me, Miss, I ain't allowed no one near me but Tom, and then 'im only because 'e said 'e'd wed me.'

'And so he shall,' declared Eustacia. 'He shall be *made* to marry you.'

'Stacey! Pray, be serious!'

'I am most serious, Rupert.'

'But he has refused to own the child!'

'I expect that was because he was frightened,' opined Eustacia, sagely. 'We must talk to him, assure him that he shall find a post where he may support his family—an even better post than his present one! Who is his present employer, Nan?'

'L-Lord Erringden.'

'Erringden?' cried Rupert. 'Why, he is one

172

of the richest men in England!'

Nan nodded. 'Tom's uncle is second footman at one of 'is lordship's 'ouses, and 'e put in a word for Tom.'

'Well, I can see that any young man would think himself fortunate to find such a position,' admitted Eustacia. 'But we must hope that he can be persuaded to own up to his obligations to this poor girl, and marry her. If that is what you would like, Nan?'

'If she would *like?* Oh by heaven!' exclaimed Rupert, striking his forehead. 'Stacey, this is madness!'

'No, no,' she said, soothingly. 'It is a tangle, I admit, but nothing we cannot solve.'

'*We?*' muttered Lady Bilderston, in failing accents.

'Why, yes, Godmama! I would have liked to track down this Mrs Bates, and punish the man responsible for Nan's injuries, but that does not seem to be possible, and so we must be thankful that we have at least saved the child, and now I shall need your help in finding a post for Nan's young man!'

*   *   *

A night's sleep did much to restore Nan's spirits, although it brought no solution to her plight. However, she was content to remain at Fanshawe Gardens, confident that Miss Marchant would soon find an answer. Eustacia pondered the problem as she joined Caroline Lagallan for their afternoon ride in the park. They soon came upon the Major and his brother, and Vivyan, noting her distracted air, asked after her protégé.

They had fallen a little way behind the others, and Eustacia glanced about her to make sure they were not overheard before giving Mr Lagallan a full account of Nan's adventures.

'The poor child is still in some discomfort, and her eye is badly swollen, but she is very much better this morning. I left her shelling peas under Cook's watchful eye.'

'And you plan to marry her off to this Tom? I wish you luck there!'

'You think it an impossible task? Perhaps, but I think that once Tom becomes used to the idea that he is to be a father, he will regret sending Nan away.' Her brow wrinkled. 'My biggest problem is to find him a suitable post, if Nan is correct that his present employer won't allow him to marry. Godmama does not require another footman, and in any case I do not think London is the best place to bring up a baby; I would prefer to find them something in the country. I have written to Grandpapa, asking him to make enquiries in the neighbourhood, but I cannot expect to hear back for some time yet.'

'I am surprised you have not asked me to help you place them.'

Her eyes flew to his face, but she was reassured by the gleam in his dark eyes, and returned his smile.

'You have done so much for me already, Vivyan. I vowed I would not trouble you with this. Unless, of course, *you* are looking for a footman?'

'No, brat, I am not! But you and young Alleyne will be setting up your own establishment very soon, will you not? You will be sure to need extra staff'

Eustacia frowned.

'Perhaps,' she said doubtfully, remembering Rupert's behaviour the previous evening. 'However, I would much rather have Tom and Nan settled before then.'

Mr Lagallan smiled down at her.

'You are working very hard on behalf of this maid, Stacey.'

'She reminds me of what might have become of *me*,' she replied in a low voice. 'Nan came to London to find Tom, and arrived penniless, friendless—very much like my own case, if you had not happened by.' She looked up, a smile trembling on her lips. 'I owe you so much, my friend.'

For a long moment green eyes held black, and she felt her breath catch in her throat. Her heart began to pound heavily as she read the message in his intense gaze.

'Eustacia—'

Mr Lagallan was interrupted by a cheery

175

voice hailing him, and Mr MacCauley trotted up.

'Well met, Viv, my friend! And Miss Marchant, your most obedient servant, ma'am!'

Mr Lagallan glared at him. 'Well, Nathan?'

Mr MacCauley's smile did not falter.

'Couldn't ride by without a word, my friend!' His grey eyes narrowed. 'I trust I am not interrupting anything?'

Eustacia felt her cheeks grow hot.

'Not at all,' replied Vivyan, in his easy style, moving forward to shield Eustacia from MacCauley's gaze. 'So have you settled your affairs now, Nathan?'

'Aye, almost. Been with the lawyers all morning—dashed officious breed! Wanted proof positive of my identity before they would part with a penny. Not that there's a great deal, when all's said—' He broke off, glancing apologetically at Miss Marchant. 'But you don't want to listen to me prosing on about these legal matters! Suffice it to say that I have a snug little property in Dorset. I am a man of substance, Viv, like yourself!'

Mr Lagallan returned a non-committal answer, and after a few more moments Mr MacCauley touched his hat and trotted off, Miss Marchant gazing thoughtfully after him. Vivyan glanced at her.

'I mistrust that look, Stacey. What plans are you hatching now?'

A pair of green eyes turned innocently towards him.

'Nothing, sir! Only . . . a property in Dorset! Do you think perhaps he will be requiring more servants?'

'No!' Mr Lagallan frowned at her. 'Stacey, I forbid you to foist that young woman and her beau on to Nathan MacCauley! He's an adventurer, m'dear. Best leave well alone.'

'So, too, were *you* an adventurer,' she reminded him.

'But I, my dear, have the advantage of a considerable fortune. Unless I am very much mistaken, Nathan MacCauley will have little to show of his inheritance once he has settled his bills in Town. He has been living pretty high, you know.'

'So you think he cannot help me?'

'I *know* it! Besides, you don't even know yet if this Tom will agree to your plans.'

*   *   *

Eustacia was well aware of that fact, and it was with some trepidation that she escorted Nan to the little gardens to meet her beau later that week. With the aid of one of Lady Bilderston's footmen acting as a messenger, and a handful of silver coins, Miss Marchant had persuaded Tom to meet Nan on his free afternoon. As she took Nan to the gardens, she spotted a thin young man pacing up and down one of the walks. She guessed his identity before Nan had uttered his name, and restrained her companion from running to meet him.

'Wait, child. We do not want to frighten him away.'

The young man eyed them warily as they approached, but Eustacia put on her most friendly smile to greet him.

'You must be Tom. I am delighted to meet you. Nan has told me all about you.'

Tom flushed, and stammered something inaudible. She continued, 'You know that Nan is going to have your child?' A hunted look appeared in the slightly protuberant blue eyes. 'It is your child, is it not? Pray tell me the truth, for believe me I only want to help you.'

He hung his head. 'Yes'm.'

'Then do you not think you should marry Nan?'

'I should o'course, but I can't! 'Is lordship'd cast me off if 'e was to find out. Strict, 'e is, and don't allow none of 'is under-staff to be wed.'

'Well, what if I was to find you a suitable post with some other gentleman? One who would not object to your having a wife. Would you marry Nan then?'

'Ah, s'pose I might do,' he said slowly. 'If I could be sure it was as good a position as this'n.'

Nan gave a loud sigh. 'Oh, Tom!'

He looked at her, a shy smile lighting his

rather vacant features. He held his hand out.

'I'm sorry, Nan, 'bout what I said t'other night. I was afeard, y'see.'

Nan hugged him. 'Course you was, Tom. I understands *that*.'

Miss Marchant turned away a little to inspect a colourful flower-bed, giving the two young people a little time to become reconciled. However, after a lengthy period she gently reminded Nan that they should be getting back. The young couple clung together for a final embrace, then Tom gently pushed the girl away from him.

'Go on now, off you go with Miss,' he said. He glanced up. 'And you'll find me a place where Nan and me can be together—a place in a gentleman's 'ouse?'

'Of course I will.' Eustacia firmly suppressed her doubts. She guided Nan back through the gardens, cudgelling her brains to hit upon some scheme for their salvation.

'We must find someone who can employ the both of you,' she told Nan. 'What can you do, child?'

'Well, Miss, I dunno.' Nan thought for a moment, then she said: 'I can milk cows!'

Eustacia's spirits sagged.

'I was thinking of something more genteel for you, such as a lady's maid.'

'I never met no ladies afore, Miss, 'cepting yourself.'

'Well, never mind. What else can you do—

179

what did you do at home, did you help your mama?'

'Why, yes'm. Mam was always poorly, so I helped with the babes, and cooked, and kept house.'

'Well, now, that is *much* better!' remarked Eustacia, brightening. 'I have no doubt we will be able to find a household where you can both be useful.'

Nan nodded, smiling up at her so trustingly that Eustacia knew she would not rest until she had secured the future for these young lovers.

*   *   *

Walking Snuffles the next morning, Eustacia pondered the problem but could find no answer. She wondered if she should ask Rupert to help her, but immediately abandoned the idea. Mr Alleyne had been noticeably cool about her adoption of Nan, and had argued strongly that the girl should be returned to her home where she should throw herself upon the mercy of the Parish. Miss Marchant's tentative suggestion that Nan and Tom could join *their* household once they were married so appalled Mr Alleyne that Eustacia had hastily disclaimed, but Rupert's lack of understanding convinced her that they should *not* marry.

She was quite sure now that she did not love Rupert, but how was she to tell him so, when he was determined upon the match? She had been about to confess everything when her grandfather interrupted them, and once Rupert had declared himself to Sir Jasper she felt as if there was no escape from the match, especially with Sir Jasper so in favour of it. The only flicker of light was that there had been no formal announcement, but even so it seemed that everyone knew their secret. To cry off now would bring hurt and disappointment to all those she loved most, including Rupert, unless he could be brought to see that they were not suited.

She was deep in thought as she entered the little park, and did not see Mr MacCauley waiting just inside the gates until she had unclipped the dog-leash and Snuffles had trotted off to enjoy his customary exploration of the gardens. The gentleman was walking towards her, smiling, and her heart sank, for she very much wanted to be alone. To turn and leave was unthinkable: Snuffles was so used to the walk now that it was unlikely he would return to her until they had completed the circuit. Bracing herself, Eustacia gave no more than a slight smile to the gentleman, and glanced behind her to assure herself that her maid was in close attendance.

'Miss Marchant! Your servant, ma'am!'

'How do you do, Mr MacCauley?'

'Very well, ma'am, thank you. But I have not seen you here recently—I had begun to think you were avoiding me!'

'I cannot tarry, sir, for I promised Lady Bilderston I would attend her—'

'And I would not detain you for the world, ma'am! I will merely accompany you on your walk.'

Miss Marchant shook her head. 'That is kind of you, sir, but truly, I prefer to walk alone this morning.'

His brows drew together. 'My dear ma'am, what has wrought this change in you? If I have in some way offended—'

'No, no, Mr MacCauley, I assure you it is nothing like that! Merely that I wish to be alone.'

But the gentleman was not to be put off. He fell into step beside her.

'Now, my dear Miss Marchant, we are such good friends that I cannot think you will object if I walk with you, especially when I tell you that I have made the acquaintance of a friend of yours—Mr Rupert Alleyne.' He returned her startled look with a bland smile. 'Yes, quite so. We met at The Cocoa Tree a few nights ago. A very pleasant young man, Mr Alleyne, and one who enjoys the patronage of Mr Lagallan, I believe.'

Eustacia was cautious.

'They are acquainted, I know no more than that,' she said.

'Mr Alleyne is fortunate to have such a friend.' Mr MacCauley's smile became more fixed. 'A man could do a great deal with someone like Mr Lagallan to recommend him.' He switched his gaze back to Eustacia. 'And now I understand that you are to marry Mr Alleyne.'

Eustacia felt her cheeks flame, and saw the triumphant look in Nathan MacCauley's eyes. She said, with as much cold dignity as she could muster: 'You are mistaken, sir!'

'Am I? True, there has been no announcement, but neither is it public knowledge that you came to London to find Mr Alleyne.'

She stopped, the colour draining from her face as quickly as it had come.

She tried to laugh. 'That is nonsense! I have no idea where you heard such a tale.'

She set off again, quickening her pace, but the gentleman fell into step beside her once more.

'Can you not guess? I had it from Mr Alleyne himself. Oh, don't worry, my dear, I have not told anyone else, but our dear young friend was banged up to the eyes by the time we left The Cocoa Tree. He was so full of wine that I had to give him my arm to get him home safe. Quite maudlin he became, telling me how unworthy he is of your undying devotion, and how you ran away from home and persuaded Mrs Lagallan to bring you to London.'

Miss Marchant tossed her head. 'I think you have said quite enough, sir. Please leave me!'

'I wonder how he would feel if he learned that it was *not* Mrs Lagallan who brought you to London,' he leaned closer and whispered, 'but her rakish brother-in-law?'

Eustacia was so startled by this that she dropped the dog-leash. Mr MacCauley retrieved it for her, a knowing smile curving his lips.

'Well, well, my dear—will you deny that, too?'

'Of course I deny it!' she said, coldly. 'What—what a preposterous idea!'

'Perhaps I should take this—ah—*preposterous* idea to Mr Alleyne? And then, of course, there is Miss Pensford to consider. Rumour has it she is about to become engaged to the gentleman in question.'

Eustacia hesitated, then she dismissed her maid, telling her that Mr MacCauley would see her home.

'Not, of course, that there is any truth in this nonsense,' she told him, 'but servants can be such tattle-mongers.'

'I quite understand you, my dear, and such a story as this could be very damaging if it became known, could it not?'

'It would be denied, of course.'

'Oh? And what about the little matter of the landlords at Marlborough and Reading, and at The Golden Cockerel?' He saw the startled look, and triumph flashed in his eyes. 'Once I had heard Mr Alleyne's tale I made enquiry, and found that Vivyan Lagallan and his—er—cousin had stopped overnight at a certain hostelry in Marlborough, and then of course I met this self-same *cousin* at The Star in Reading, and again at The Golden Cockerel. How could I forget the tender touch that soothed my fevered brow through the night?'

Eustacia put up her chin. 'That is no concern of mine, I assure you.'

'Strange, then, that this cousin should bear such a striking resemblance to yourself—the red hair and green eyes. Very remarkable, and well remembered by the landlords at these hostelries. And I know from my enquiries, Miss Marchant, that Vivyan Lagallan *has* no cousin matching that description! A fine tale to take to Miss Pensford.'

Miss Marchant frowned.

'What do you want?'

'Just a little of what is due to me, a place in society. You know that Lagallan and I were travelling-companions a few years ago. Neither of us had a penny to scratch with, yet here he is now, the darling of the *ton*, courted wherever he goes—what harm would it have done him to introduce me to his world? But no, he refused me, and yet he has taken that boy Alleyne under his wing, introduced him to his clubs—it should be me, *me* receiving such favours, not that pup!' He broke off, his face working as he considered the injustice of his situation, then he said in a calmer tone, 'But

185

you don't want to hear me ranting in this way.'

'No, sir, I do not. All I know is that your dangerous lies could be very injurious to—to people whom I hold in affection. I would like to avoid that.'

'Good, that's very sensible of you, Miss Marchant. I knew we would deal together.' He reached out to touch her arm, but she snatched it away as if she had been burned.

'So, what is it you want—money? I have little enough of that, I assure you.'

'Money, well, that would be welcome, but—no, more than that.' MacCauley paused. 'I want an entrée to Society.'

She laughed at him.

'But how can I help you there? I might be able to persuade my godmother to introduce you to one or two of her friends, but—'

'Oh no, my dear, that would not do at all. No, I have thought it all out. I want you to marry me.'

CHAPTER THIRTEEN

Eustacia stopped in her tracks and turned to stare at Nathan MacCauley, then she threw back her head and laughed. The gentleman regarded her patiently, his own good humour unimpaired.

'Mock me all you want, my dear, but

consider: if I take this story to Rupert Alleyne, do you think he will marry you, once he knows that you were traipsing all over the country dressed as a boy, the mistress of Vivyan Lagallan?'

Her eyes flashing with rage, Eustacia brought her hand up and struck him once, hard across the face. MacCauley flinched, but his sneering smile did not falter.

'That is not true!' she exclaimed.

'No?' he purred. 'Once I have told my tale, there are enough clues, enough little details that I know to make Society question, and then doubt. Even if Mr Alleyne is besotted with you, do you think his father would allow the wedding to go ahead? Much better that he thinks you have changed your mind, than that he should ever know the truth, eh?' He paused to allow his words to sink in. 'And then we come to Miss Pensford. A very genteel girl, I understand, from a family that abhors scandal. Such a deal of unpleasantness, and with your assistance we could avoid it all. Come, Miss Marchant—Eustacia! We have grown to know each other quite well, have we not? You may not love me now, but I am a considerate man, and you will not find me ungenerous. Once I am established, I am even prepared to let you go your own way, as long as you are discreet.'

Miss Marchant dragged her scattered wits together, trying to think rationally. She said scornfully: 'If, *if* I were to give up Mr Alleyne and marry you, I should very likely be cut off without a penny, without a friend. After all, you have not always been respectable, have you?'

His smile did not reassure her.

'Perhaps not, but you would find it difficult to prove, my dear. The only evidence that could have harmed me was in the letters you so kindly retrieved for me.' His smile deepened unpleasantly as Stacey paled. 'Oh, I know, you wish now that you had kept them, do you not? But you may be sure that I destroyed those letters before I left The Golden Cockerel. My past is now as clear as, shall we say, Vivyan Lagallan's.

'I have no doubt that your family will be angry at first, but I watched you driving out with your grandfather, and walking here, in this very garden. It is clear he dotes on you. I have no doubt you could persuade him to make the best of it. After all, I am not ineligible, you know. I have my property in Dorset. Mayhap my wealth is not as great as Mr Alleyne's, but Sir Jasper would no more want this story published than Lagallan, would he?'

'You would not tell him!'

'Well, my dear, that very much depends upon yourself. If you wish, you may give him to understand that you mistook your heart. I don't think the old man would wish you to be miserable.'

They had arrived back at the gateway, and Snuffles was now trotting up to Eustacia, expecting the usual titbit. Miss Marchant bent to clip the leash on to the dog's collar. 'I—I need time to consider.'

Mr MacCauley shrugged, and thought of his creditors, whose letters and bills were filling several drawers of his desk.

'I will give you until next Saturday.'

'But that is barely a week!'

'That should be long enough for you to decide, and for me to obtain a special licence. I know you have attained your majority, so there'll be no need for a flight to the border!' He grinned at her. 'I will expect you here on Saturday morning, with an answer.'

Then, with a flourishing bow, he lounged away, whistling.

*　　　*　　　*

Feeling physically sick, Eustacia hurried back to Lady Bilderston's house and locked herself in her room. Considering the situation, she realized she was much more angry than afraid. If she had been carrying a pistol, she thought she would have shot Nathan MacCauley there and then, with very little remorse. This pleasant vision occupied her thoughts for a few moments, but then she turned her mind to find a more practical way out of her difficulties. None occurred. Her first impulse was to turn to Vivyan, but he had taken Caroline and the children to Worthing. Besides, she was not sure that he *could* help her: if he challenged Nathan MacCauley to a duel, it was certain that MacCauley would make sure the story was known beforehand, and then the damage would be even worse! She considered confessing everything to Rupert, but he would be so horrified she quaked at the very thought of his reaction. No, she thought miserably, she must find a solution for herself.

*   *   *

She was no further forward when Wednesday arrived, and she prepared for Lady Bilderston's party with a feeling of impending doom. She knew she was looking wan, and pinched her cheeks until they were stinging, but to no avail. Lady Bilderston attributed her god-daughter's lack of spirits to too many late nights.

'I have been so diverted by your visit that I have failed to make sure you had sufficient rest. And now you have brought that—that young person into the house, causing mayhem—'

'Oh, dear,' exclaimed Eustacia. 'Is Nan very troublesome?'

'Well, no,' conceded my lady. 'In fact, Cook says she is a good girl, and very handy about the kitchen, but you know what I mean! I cannot keep her here, my love, and heaven knows I cannot think of anyone of my acquaintance who would take her, in her condition!'

'Oh, Godmama, how tiresome of me to foist her on to you! But you must not trouble yourself about Nan, for I am determined to find a suitable placement for her and Tom.' She hugged Lady Bilderston, heedless of that lady's protests not to crush her gown. 'You are the best of godmothers, ma'am!'

'Yes, yes, but that does not change the fact that you are looking very pale, my love, and that will not do. We will not go to Almack's tomorrow, and perhaps we should cry off from Lady Addingham's ball on Saturday. A few days' rest will restore your spirits, I am sure. Now, what do you say?'

Thinking of her forthcoming meeting with Nathan MacCauley, Eustacia could only nod: suddenly she would have given everything to be safely back in Somerset, and to find that all this had been a dream. But it was real, and Eustacia knew her duty: she stood with her godmother at the top of the sweeping staircase and greeted the guests, smiling and chatting as if she had not a care in the world.

When Rupert arrived, he kissed her cheek dutifully, failed to notice her unnatural pallor and wandered off to mingle with the rest of the guests. Miss Pensford arrived shortly after, with her parents, and Eustacia observed that

Mrs Pensford had thrown off her mourning-clothes and was wearing a very elegant gown of blue satin, several shades darker than the celestial-blue lustring of her daughter's robe, but equally expensive. As if to add to her depression, Eustacia realized that if Mrs Pensford had now ended her mourning for her cousin, there was little to prevent the announcement of Miss Pensford's engagement to Vivyan. Such lowering thoughts did nothing to lighten Eustacia's mood, but she covered it well, and no one talking to Miss Marchant would have guessed the turmoil within.

Soon after supper, she entered the salon and saw Rupert and Helen Pensford sitting together, deep in conversation. When at last Rupert moved away, Miss Pensford's eyes followed him, and there was such a look of longing and despair on her usually impassive countenance that Eustacia felt her stomach turn over. It seemed impossible to Eustacia that Helen should prefer Rupert to Vivyan. A sudden realization burst upon her: she could scarcely believe it. She told herself it was impossible, but the idea, once born, was not to be brushed aside lightly. Excusing herself from the next dance, much to the chagrin of her partner, Eustacia slipped between the chattering spectators and watched. It soon became apparent that Mr Alleyne's eyes strayed far too frequently towards Miss Pensford, and when he spoke to her, that young lady's pale cheek became suffused with a delicate blush.

'Of course,' muttered Eustacia. 'What a fool I have been not to see it before!' A mischievous twinkle gleamed in her eyes: it was now even more necessary to rescue Vivyan, and make two other people happy at the same time!

*   *   *

The following morning found Miss Marchant in a whirl of activity, and by the time she took Snuffles for his morning walk, she had already sent Nan upon an errand and arranged for her groom to bring her mare to the door at noon. Lady Bilderston, coming out of her bedroom just as Eustacia was descending the stairs, expressed her amazement at her god-daughter's energy.

'Surely you are not riding at this hour?' she exclaimed, observing Eustacia's riding-dress.

'Why, yes, ma'am.' Eustacia glanced down at the bandbox she carried in one gloved hand. 'I—um—I discovered a rent in one of my gowns, and I thought I would drop it in to Madame Sylvie while I am out today.'

'My dear child, if you have torn a gown there is no need to bother the modiste with it. Let me take it, and my woman shall set a stitch in it directly—' She reached out to take the bandbox, but Eustacia whipped it away.

193

'No, no, it—it is far too bad to be repaired here! I am sorry, Godmama, I did not wish to tell you, but I see I must confess. I caught it on a splinter when I was in the garden last week, and it is quite ripped! I was hoping to have it repaired before you knew anything about it. Pray, ma'am, let me do this, or I shall never forgive myself.' On these words Eustacia ran lightly down the stairs, stopping at the bottom to blow her godmother a kiss before she danced out of the house.

Shaking her head, Lady Bilderston made her way downstairs at a more sedate pace, muttering under her breath about the unpredictability of her god-daughter.

*　　　*　　　*

On Saturday morning Mr MacCauley was waiting within the gardens for Eustacia, and as she approached he made his bow, then turned to walk beside her.

'Well, Miss Marchant—do you have an answer?'

She ignored his proffered arm.

'First, tell me something of your property in Dorset. Is—is it a large estate?'

Mr MacCauley drew himself up.

'Large enough. There is the home farm, and several acres of woodland. Haven't seen it for years, but I doubt if it has changed much. My uncle did not enjoy good health, I understand,

194

and the property has been run by his agent for the past dozen years.'

'So it will have servants, footmen and chambermaids, and the like?'

'By heaven, yes! I ain't a pauper, you know.'

'Then yes, I have decided to accept your offer—to buy your silence!'

'A wise decision, my dear, if I may say so. Well, there's a little church in Highgate. As soon as I've made all right with the curate—'

'Pray, sir, let me finish! There are . . . *terms.*'

He frowned at her, suddenly wary.

'Terms?'

'Yes. I am attending Lady Addingham's ball this evening, and I want you to bring a travelling-coach to the door at eleven o'clock. From there we will travel to The Sun at Frith, where I have already secured rooms for us, and sent on my luggage—'

'And why all this havey-cavey business, Miss? If you're agreeable to marrying me, why don't we just come out and tell your godmother?'

'Because Mr Alleyne is very likely to shoot you, when he learns I have rejected him for you!' She added mendaciously, 'And I understand that he is a crack shot, too. No, it will be better if we tie the knot *before* we tell my family. And you need not think there will be any impropriety—my maid will be in attendance.'

'Well, I don't like it! How do I know you

195

won't double-cross me?'

'You have my word upon it!' She fixed him with her direct gaze. 'You *can* arrange a carriage for tonight, can you not?'

'Well, of course I can, but I can't help thinking there's something dashed smoky about this whole thing!'

It took Miss Marchant some time to persuade Nathan MacCauley to agree to her plan, but her success elated her, and when she walked into Lady Bilderston's morning-room some half an hour later, her eyes were still shining with her triumph.

'Stacey, my love, have you been out already? I thought you were going to rest today.' Lady Bilderston was seated at the little writing-desk, but now she leaned down to pat Snuffles, who had trotted up to her, flanks heaving from his exertion, but his tail wagging in greeting.

'I am feeling so much better today, Godmama! In fact, I have asked Merlow to bring Bianca round in twenty minutes.'

'My dear child, you cannot be thinking of riding today!'

'Why not? I am not in the least tired now. You must not fret, ma'am, I shall be back in plenty of time to prepare for tonight's party.'

'Oh, but I was this minute writing to Lady Addingham with our apologies. I had quite forgotten to tell her that we would not be attending.' She saw Eustacia's blank look, and added: 'You will remember that we decided we would forgo the party tonight, for you were looking so worn out, and when I suggested we should rest you agreed—'

'Oh, heavens, did I really? Pray do not send it!' cried Eustacia. 'Dear ma'am, I have promised so many people that I shall be there, I could not possibly cry off?'

'But, my dear, you have been looking so pale of late—'

'But I am not pale now, Godmama, am I?'

'Well, no, but—'

Eustacia fell to her knees before her godmother and clutched at her hands.

'*Dearest* Godmama, pray tell me that we may go! I have been so looking forward to this ball, and besides, you yourself told me you wanted to wear the new lilac crepe that so becomes you, and what better occasion than this!'

'Oh . . . very well, if you have set your heart on it, my love, but after this, you must promise me you will give up at least some of your engagements. If you go home looking positively haggard your grandfather will lay the blame at my door.'

Eustacia felt the hot tears pricking at her eyes.

'You may be easy, then,' she said. 'I promise you, everything will change after this evening!'

*　　　*　　　*

With so much to plan and organize, Miss Marchant wasted no time in fruitless speculation about the future, and an hour later she was trotting across Westminster Bridge and following her groom south on the Brighton road.

Nan's visit to Bruton Street the previous day had elicited the information that Mr Lagallan would be returning directly to London from Worthing, and was expected to arrive in town mid-afternoon. Her groom assured her that she was travelling on the main route into Town, and she could only hope that nothing had occurred to change Mr Lagallan's plans. She passed the turnpike at St George's, trotted quickly past the asylum, and set off across Kennington Common. As the last of the houses disappeared, her groom brought his horse alongside hers, looking nervously about him.

'There is no need to worry, Merlow,' she remarked with more confidence than she felt. 'Surely it is much too early for highwaymen?'

'I'd be happier if we was back in the town, Miss.'

'And we will bc, hopefully, before too long! You did say this is the main road from Worthing, is it not?'

'Aye, Miss, it is, but why you should want to ride out so far is a mystery to me.'

'And so it shall remain, but not for much longer, I hope, for I am growing uncomfortably hot!'

'Well, that's hardly a surprise, Miss, if I may say so!' declared Merlow, casting an eloquent glance at the heavy redingote she was wearing over her riding-habit. Feeling the sun on his own back, Merlow looked up at the cloudless blue sky and silently shook his head at the mysterious ways of the gentry. Ignoring him, Miss Marchant squinted into the distance, putting up one hand to shield her eyes from the sun.

'Is—is that a coach coming towards us? I—I think . . . yes!'

She sighed with relief as she recognized Mr Lagallan's high-stepping bays. The carriage was approaching at speed, and she brought her mare to a halt in the middle of the highway, waving frantically at the coachman.

The horses checked, and as the equipage came to a halt she saw Vivyan's dark head appear at the window. Throwing the reins to her groom, Eustacia slipped easily to the ground.

'Good afternoon, Vivyan! How fortunate I should come across you.'

'Is it?' Mr Lagallan's dark eyes glinted at her as he jumped down from the carriage, but she met his suspicious gaze with her own innocent look.

'I have been exploring, you see, but the sun is so hot, and I had just begun to feel a little faint.'

'Well, no wonder at it, when you are wearing that dashed heavy surcoat! Here, let me help you take it off.'

'I thought it might rain,' she murmured, not meeting his eyes as she unbuttoned the coat.

'Then you would have done better to stay at home!' he retorted.

She did not reply, but swayed slightly against him. His face softened.

'Come along then, brat, you'd better let me take you back.'

In a fading voice, Eustacia instructed Merlow to take her mare back to the stable, and allowed Mr Lagallan to help her into the carriage. Vivyan threw the offending surcoat on to the seat then climbed in beside her. Eustacia glanced at him from under her lashes, noting his stern expression.

'It is very good of you to come to my assistance.'

'It is my pleasure, ma'am.'

She began to pull off her gloves. 'You are *angry* with me: you always become punctilious when I have offended you.'

'You should not be here, alone in the carriage with me. What tricks are you playing now, Stacey?'

'None, I assure you. Is Caroline quite settled in Worthing?'

'Yes. She and the boys are comfortable enough. She has some thoughts of buying a house there, and plans to start looking for a

200

suitable property once Philip joins them at the end of the month.'

'And will you go back?'

'No. I have an appointment with Miss Pensford's father tomorrow, to draft out the notice of our engagement.'

There was an uncomfortable silence. Eustacia's eyes roamed around the coach, looking everywhere except at her host—at the thickly padded squabs, the carriage-pistols gleaming in their leather holsters, the polished brass handles on the doors. Aware that Vivyan was watching her, she closed her eyes and pretended to sleep. The carriage rattled on, and she heard him sigh.

'What a damnable coil!'

She did not move, but her heart went out to him: she was more determined than ever that her plan must succeed.

*   *   *

As the carriage pulled into Fanshawe Gardens, Eustacia stirred and opened her eyes.

'Oh, are we here so soon?'

Vivyan was already jumping down from the carriage. Eustacia rose and shook out her skirts, and as she did so her fine leather gloves flew out on to the flagway.

'Oh, dear—I had forgotten they were in my lap! And my surcoat!' As Vivyan stooped to retrieve the gloves, she turned back to gather

201

up her coat before descending from the carriage.

With her coat draped over one arm, and her gloves held tightly in her free hand, Eustacia could only smile at Vivyan.

'Forgive me if I do not shake hands with you, but pray believe that I am truly grateful to you for helping me! Will I see you at Lady Addingham's tonight?'

'No, I think not.'

Eustacia digested this information with no visible signs of disappointment: in fact, it suited her better that she would not have Vivyan's percipient gaze upon her that evening. She looked up at him, trying to fix every detail of his dear face in her memory.

'Goodbye, Vivyan.' She hesitated, as if she would say more, then turned and ran lightly into the house.

*   *   *

It was not to be expected that Lady Bilderston would remain in ignorance of Eustacia's return in Mr Lagallan's carriage, but Eustacia waved aside her godmother's concerns and insisted upon preparing for the party, declaring that she had never felt better in her life. Lady Bilderston could not deny that her god-daughter was indeed in quite her best looks; there was a healthy glow to her cheeks, and her green eyes sparkled as she sat before her mirror while her maid skilfully fixed a number of creamy rosebuds amongst her curls.

Lady Bilderston looked a little perturbed when Miss Marchant came downstairs with her thick travelling-cloak over her arm, but if she preferred to shroud herself in its heavy folds rather than a more elegant silk wrap, my lady felt unequal to the task of arguing. Instead, she merely shrugged her plump shoulders and led the way to the waiting coach.

*   *   *

Later, in the grand ballroom of Addingham House, Lady Bilderston watched her god-daughter whirling around the dance-floor, and had to admit that the child showed no signs of her earlier malaise. Indeed, she thought she had rarely seen her so animated, laughing at Mr Alleyne who, by contrast, was looking unusually solemn. Lady Bilderston thought, too, that Miss Pensford was not in her best looks, but that might have been due to Mr Lagallan's absence. Rumour had it that the couple were about to announce their engagement, so it was no wonder if the poor child was missing her beau!

Miss Pensford's lack of spirits had not escaped Eustacia's notice as she moved through the dance, and she remarked upon it to Rupert, asking in a teasing voice if he had quarrelled with her.

'I? No, of course not!' replied that gentleman, startled. The dance had ended, and he glanced over Eustacia's head towards Miss Pensford. 'Perhaps—perhaps I should speak to her, just to ensure that I have not unwittingly been uncivil.'

Miss Marchant's green eyes gleamed. She said solemnly, 'Yes, I think that's a good idea, Rupert.' Noting his worried look, her own eyes softened, and after a moment she said, 'But before you do so, I think we should talk. Come with me, Rupert, it is important.' She led him towards the tall windows that opened out on to the terrace. 'Let us step out into the garden, where we may be private.'

'Stacey, I am not sure we should,' murmured Rupert, hanging back. 'The proprieties—'

'Oh, to the devil with the proprieties! It's too late for me now!' she added quietly to herself, thinking of her plans for later that evening. She tugged at his hand. 'Believe me, Rupert, this is very important! Pray don't be prudish.'

She dragged him down the shallow steps and into one of the shadowed walks that ran off at each side of the wide lawn. The clear sky was darkening, and the first stars twinkled above them. Only when Eustacia was sure they were alone did she stop and turn towards him. She stared up at him, meeting his puzzled look with her own determined gaze.

'Rupert, I think it is time for the truth. I am releasing you from our engagement.'

Even in the dim light his confusion was evident. 'R-releasing me? I—I don't understand.'

'Dear Rupert, I am sorry, but I find I don't love you, after all.' She gave a little sigh. 'When we were in Somerset, I was sure I did—I think you swept me off my feet! But—but once I arrived in London, everything changed.'

'Stacey, there is no need for this! You are confused, perhaps, because everything has happened so quickly.' Rupert took her hands, giving her a tight smile. 'Have I been a little distant recently? I am sorry—I promise you, I don't mean to cry off.'

'Oh, how kind you are, *dear* Rupert! But we should not suit, you see. I am far too careless of convention for your taste, I know that, and you—well, you deserve better than to be tied to someone who cannot make you happy.' She squeezed his hands before letting them go. 'I have known for some time that my feelings have changed: I was going to tell you the day my grandfather came to London, but—but once you had declared yourself, and Grandpapa accepted so readily, I was too much overcome to tell you! But now—well, I know it would never work out, and I am releasing you.'

'Stacey, I—I don't know what to say . . .' Rupert ran his hands through his carefully disordered locks. 'My dear—if I have given you cause to think—'

'No, no, you have been most punctilious in your attentions, but I do not love you, and you, I think—no, I am certain—your heart belongs to another.' She smiled at his swift protest. 'No, don't deny it, Rupert. You love Helen, do you not?'

For a long moment Rupert said nothing, then with a sigh he turned away and, sinking down on to a low wall, he dropped his head into his hands.

'With all my heart,' he groaned. 'We—I had hoped to conceal it from you.'

'Don't reproach yourself, Rupert. Perhaps if I had not fallen out of love with you, I would not have seen it. And Helen loves you, too, does she not?'

He sighed. 'I—yes. But it cannot be. She is to marry Lagallan.'

Eustacia sat beside him on the wall, and placed a hand on his shoulder.

'You must persuade her to cry off.'

'She will not.'

'But, Rupert, you must try! I know Mr and Mrs Pensford would not wish her to marry against her heart. And you are not ineligible; your fortune may be less than Vivyan's, but you are not a pauper!'

He shook his head. 'Helen—Miss Pensfold—has a strong sense of duty.'

'*Duty!*' exclaimed Eustacia. 'There is no love

206

between them; Vivyan knows that, but he cannot—will not—cry off, knowing how ruinous that would be to Helen's reputation! Helen must be persuaded, Rupert. If she doesn't love Vivyan, it is wrong of her to make him unhappy!'

Rupert raised his head and looked at her, sudden understanding dawning in his eyes.

'So that's it! By God, it's Lagallan you care for!'

'If Helen marries him, all three of you will be unhappy!'

'But would you be quite so concerned if Vivyan Lagallan was not involved?' He read the answer in her eyes. 'Devil take it, Stacey, surely you don't think he will marry *you?*'

She flinched at the incredulous note in his voice.

'Of course not, but I will do anything within my power to spare him pain. Persuade Helen to cry off, Rupert; there is no sensible reason why you two should not be happy.'

He looked at her. 'Do you think so, truly?'

She smiled. 'Truly.' She gave him a little push. 'Go and find her now.'

She followed Mr Alleyne back into the ballroom, and watched as he made his way to Miss Pensford. He spoke to her, then they moved back to sit on a small sofa that had been placed in one of the alcoves. Even from a distance, Eustacia could see that they were in earnest conversation, their fair heads close

together, and she held her breath, willing
Rupert to succeed, but after a few moments
Rupert jumped to his feet. Miss Pensford
averted her face, and raised one white hand in
a gesture of dismissal. Rupert, his lips tightly
compressed, stalked away.

Miss Marchant quickly intercepted him.

'Well? What did she say?'

He looked down at her, his face flushed
with anger, and for some moments his angry
gaze looked straight through her.

'Rupert?'

'What? Oh—she is not to be moved. Stacey,
I—I am very grateful for what you have done
in releasing me from our betrothal, but—but it
is not to be expected that Miss Pensford could
cry off from an engagement! It is not in her
nature to act in—in such an unladylike
manner.'

Eustacia stared at him, then an angry flush
rose over her face.

'You imply that *I* have done so, in fact?'

'That is not what I meant!'

'It is *exactly* what you meant!' she flashed,
blinking away angry tears. 'Oh, go away,
Rupert! I might have been unladylike, but I
cannot regret jilting you!' She turned on her
heel and walked off, not pausing until she had
reached the relative calm of the main landing.
She leaned against the balustrade, breathing
deeply to regain her temper. How dare he?
When her actions had saved him from a

loveless marriage! For some minutes she continued to rage inwardly, but gradually common sense reasserted itself. The clock in the hall below began to chime: ten o'clock! Since Rupert had failed to persuade Helen to cry off, she would have to try what she could do to free Vivyan from a disastrous match.

*   *   *

Miss Pensford was dancing when Eustacia went back into the ballroom, but it was clear to anyone who knew her well that the young lady was not enjoying herself. As the music stopped, Eustacia waited for the couples to disperse, then went up to Miss Pensford, saying brightly: 'There you are, Helen! I have been looking for you. Pray step aside with me for a moment, that we may talk.'

Miss Pensford gave her a curious glance, but allowed herself to be guided into a small side chamber which was empty save for one aged dowager dozing on a sofa. Eustacia softly closed the door.

'You know—Rupert has told you—that we are no longer engaged?'

Miss Pensford drew away a little.

'Yes, and I cannot condone it.'

'I would not ask that of you, but I need your help. You do not look to be enjoying the party, Helen, and neither am I. I will be leaving at eleven o'clock, and I beg you, as my friend, to come with me.'

Miss Pensford stared at her.

'Leave? But how can I? Mama—'

'You may tell Mrs Pensford that I am unwell and you are accompanying me home. Helen, please do this for me; I would not ask you if it were not imperative. Lady Bilderston is enjoying herself, and I owe her so much already that I do not wish to drag her away so early! Once we are alone, I will explain everything to you. Please say you will come with me!'

Miss Pensford's resolve wavered. She had not been hopeful of an enjoyable evening, but it had proved far, far worse than she had expected: to stay would only prolong the misery.

'Very well. I will come with you. You may set me down at my house, for it is only one block away from your own at Fanshawe Gardens.'

A delighted smile broke upon Miss Marchant's countenance. While Helen went to inform her mama that she was leaving, Eustacia left a message for Lady Bilderston and passed another note to one of the footmen, pressing a coin into his hand as she gave him detailed instructions. Then she dragged Helen down the wide staircase and called for their wraps. A small form in a red cloak appeared from the shadows near the main doors. Miss Marchant held out her hand.

'Ah, Nan, there you are. Have you brought my bag with you?'

'Yes'm.' Nan smiled worshipfully at Miss Marchant, and held out a large reticule.

'Stacey, you know this creature?' exclaimed Miss Pensford.

Eustacia's smile grew.

'Of course. I rescued Nan at Covent Garden. Did Rupert not tell you? I felt sure he would.'

'Well, yes, but—'

Miss Marchant was not listening. She turned again to Nan.

'There has been a change of plan, child. I shall not be needing you now. Take these coins—you must take a chair back to Lady Bilderston's and wait to hear from me. I shall send for you and Tom as soon as I can.'

Nan sketched a clumsy curtsy and hurried off, leaving Miss Marchant to usher her bemused friend out of the big double doors, just as the clock struck eleven.

CHAPTER FOURTEEN

Outside, there was very little traffic, but Eustacia noted that a large travelling-carriage was drawn up at the side of the road. She linked her arm through Helen's and guided her down the steps. Nathan MacCauley emerged from the carriage and held open the door.

'Well, at least you are punctual, I'll say that much for you!' he muttered.

'Who is that?' demanded Miss Pensford, hesitating.

'Only a servant,' murmured Eustacia, hurrying her friend into the carriage.

'*Servant?*' exclaimed Mr MacCauley, following them into the coach. 'This ain't your maid, I'll be bound!'

'Maid? Stacey—what is going on?' cried Miss Pensford.

The carriage began to pull away and Eustacia waited until it was moving at a smart pace before replying.

'I am running away to be married, Helen, and I need a chaperone.'

It was not to be expected that Miss Pensford would accept such an explanation with equanimity. Her jaw dropped and her eyes widened as she stared at Miss Marchant.

'Pray, Eustacia, this is no time for funning!'

'I am in earnest! I have promised to marry this gentleman, but surely you can see that I cannot travel alone with him. It would be most improper.'

Even in the darkness of the carriage, it was plain that Miss Pensford was very angry.

'How dare you treat me thus? I demand you take me back this minute!'

'Now just what is going on here?' demanded

212

Nathan MacCauley, looking from one to the other. Both ladies ignored him.

'I am afraid I cannot take you back, Helen. We are on our way to Frith. But I have every hope that Rupert will follow us there, and he will bring you back to Town.'

'R-Rupert? But—'

'You see, I left him a note, telling him where we were going.'

Nathan MacCauley leaned forward.

'You left a note for young Alleyne?'

'Yes, but you need not worry,' Eustacia told him. 'He will not be coming to save *me*.'

'Madam, we had an agreement!' he muttered, his voice deep with menace.

'Yes, and I mean to stand by it, but I told you there were conditions,' retorted Eustacia. 'I trust you have told your coachman to drive to The Sun at Frith?'

'I have, and perhaps you would tell me now why you chose that inn?'

She smiled at him.

'Because the landlord there is open to persuasion, and I have paid him very well to look after my interests this evening.'

'Bribed him, have you? Well, that's as may be but I think it's time we turned about again,' growled the gentleman. 'This looks very much like a kidnap, and *that* I don't hold with!'

'Set me down immediately!' cried Miss Pensford. 'I have no wish to go with you!'

'But you must, Helen. I have told Rupert

213

that I am going to keep you with me until you agree to call off your engagement to Vivyan.'

Nathan MacCauley stared, his eyes shifting from one young lady to the other.

'Do you mean to tell me that you have brought Viv Lagallan's fiancée with you? Are you all about in your head? He'll call me out for sure!'

'No he won't, for he knows nothing about it,' replied Stacey. She turned to Miss Pensford. 'Helen, only admit that you are in love with Rupert! Surely you can see that it would be a gross folly to go through with your marriage to Vivyan?'

Miss Pensford drew out her handkerchief. 'I would be called a *jilt*!'

'Well, since the engagement has not yet been announced, I do not see how that can be,' Miss Marchant reassured her.

'Have I strayed into Bedlam?' demanded Mr MacCauley. 'I wish you would tell me what is going on. In fact, I will put an end to this dashed nonsense now—'

'I think not.'

Even as he moved towards the window to call out to the coachman, Eustacia reached into the large reticule and pulled out a carriage-pistol.

With a little scream, Miss Pensford fell back into the corner of the carriage, and Mr MacCauley stared at the weapon gleaming wickedly in the moonlight. He shifted his gaze

214

to Eustacia's determined face.

'Wh—what is this?'

'You know very well what it is,' she replied calmly. 'It is loaded, and I have its partner also, so I would suggest you sit back quietly until we reach The Sun. And Helen, I really think you should stop crying, if you don't want Rupert to find you with your face blotched with tears.'

Miss Pensford blew her little nose defiantly, and managed to restrict her distress to the occasional sob.

The uneasy silence lasted until they reached Frith, and the carriage pulled into the cobbled yard of the inn. Responding to the largesse bestowed upon him by Miss Marchant on her previous visit, the landlord was looking out for them, and ran out in time to hand the ladies tenderly out of the coach, informing Miss Marchant with a low bow that supper had been prepared for them. He then led the three travellers into the inn, promised to bring them coffee directly, and ushered them into the private parlour.

'Well, this is very pleasant,' remarked Eustacia, looking at the table laid with pies, bread and cheese.

Miss Pensford gave a shudder, and went to sit in a chair in the far corner of the room, while Nathan MacCauley watched Eustacia, his eyes constantly moving to the folds of her cloak, where he knew she was holding

215

the pistol.

'Perhaps you would be good enough to tell me what we are going to do now?' he said, with awful sarcasm.

Unruffled, Eustacia considered the matter.

'I think we should try to eat a little supper while we wait for Rupert to arrive.'

Miss Pensford looked up from her handkerchief.

'H-how do you know he will come?'

'Because he is head over heels in love with you, you goose!'

'But you told me this young woman is engaged to Lagallan!' Mr MacCauley interjected.

'And so she is, but she loves Mr Alleyne, don't you, Helen?'

Receiving no reply, Eustacia sat down at the table, placing the pistol on the cloth beside her plate. Nathan MacCauley stared at her.

'I think, madam, that you have run mad.'

'Quite possibly, but I could not sit by and see Vivyan ruin his life. A poor friend I should be if I did not at least make a push to save him.'

Miss Pensford raised her head.

'I want to go home!' she wailed.

'And so you shall, just as soon as Rupert gets here. In the meantime, I suggest you try this ham pie—it is delicious.'

Muttering under his breath, Mr MacCauley stepped forward and banged his fist upon the table.

'Forget about pies, madam, and tell me—'

The entry of the landlady with the coffee-pot interrupted him. As the door opened, Eustacia threw her napkin over the pistol lying on the table, her eyes twinkling mischievously. She thanked her hostess politely, and as that good lady left the room, she invited her companions to join her at the table. Neither paid any heed to this request, and with a little shrug Eustacia poured the coffee into three cups and asked Mr MacCauley to carry one to Miss Pensford.

'Pray try to drink it, my dear, for it will make you feel much more the thing,' she told her.

Nathan MacCauley frowned at Miss Marchant's unconcern.

'This is not at all what I had planned, madam!'

'No, but it can make very little difference to us.'

'It will make a great deal of difference, if we are locked up for kidnap!'

'Oh, nonsense! Once Rupert has rescued Miss Pensford and taken her home, we will most likely hear no more about it, except that they will thank us one day for making them see sense!' She glanced across as Miss Pensford. 'Is that not right, Helen?'

That young lady, revived by the coffee, cast her a look of disdain.

'I merely want to go home,' she snapped.

'And what does that man mean? *What* plans have you made?'

'My apologies, I have not introduced you! This is Nathan MacCauley, Helen, and as I told you earlier we are going to be married.'

'Married? To *him*?'

Mr MacCauley bridled a little at the look of disbelief that Miss Pensford bestowed upon him.

'But surely you did not reject Mr Alleyne for *him*?'

'No, Helen, of course not. I cried off from that engagement because I didn't love Rupert. The agreement with Mr MacCauley is very different.'

'Well,' Miss Pensford pressed her, 'why *are* you marrying him?'

Eustacia hesitated, and Nathan MacCauley said maliciously, 'Shall I tell her?'

'No!' Miss Marchant's hand closed over the pistol. 'I swear I shall shoot you if you dare to speak!'

'But I don't understand,' said Miss Pensford, bewildered. 'How can you say you are going to marry this man, then threaten to shoot him?'

Feeling more sure of himself, Mr MacCauley beamed at Helen.

'I am marrying Miss Marchant to save her reputation. Is that not correct, my dear?'

Eustacia nodded.

'We have an agreement.'

'Oh, yes.' The gentleman patted his pocket. 'And I have the special licence! Tomorrow, we shall be married!'

'Eustacia, you cannot!'

Eustacia shrugged. 'It will be a marriage of convenience, Helen. I thought you would approve of that.'

'Yes, but—' She broke off, as the sound of a carriage could be heard clattering into the yard. Miss Pensford clasped her hands together, her eyes shining with hope.

'Rupert?' she uttered.

Swallowing hard, Eustacia rose from the table. A hasty step sounded in the passage. Miss Pensford rose, and took a few paces towards the door, but as it opened the hopeful look died from her eyes, to be replaced by one of horror as Vivyan Lagallan strode into the room.

CHAPTER FIFTEEN

Mr Lagallan stripped off his gloves, his mocking glance sweeping across the room. His lip lifted in a sneer as he looked at the three faces before him; each registered varying degrees of horror.

'I conclude you were not expecting me,' he drawled.

This proved too much for Miss Pensford,

and with a little moan she fainted away, to be caught by Mr MacCauley, who was standing close beside her. At that moment more footsteps were heard, and Mr Alleyne hurried in.

'I can get no sense out of that rascally landlord,' he was saying, as he entered the room. Vivyan held up a hand to stop him.

'No need. We have found our quarry.'

Mr Alleyne halted, but at that moment he saw Mr MacCauley gently placing Miss Pensford's lifeless form on the settle, and he threw himself forward, crying:

'Unhand her, you fiend!'

As Mr MacCauley stood up and turned, Mr Alleyne was upon him, landing him a flush hit to the jaw and following in with several more well-placed blows, which sent Nathan MacCauley sprawling back against the wall.

'Rupert, stop it! He was not harming her!' cried Eustacia, grabbing at his arm and holding him back from his dazed opponent. She gave him a little push.

'Go and look after Helen, do!'

Rupert needed no second bidding; he threw himself on his knees beside the settle.

'Helen, my darling,' he muttered, chafing her hands between his own. 'If he has hurt you—'

'Of course he hasn't!' snapped Eustacia, helping Mr MacCauley to his feet. 'She merely fainted. Come along, sir; let me help you to the table.'

Miss Pensford opened her eyes at that moment and saw Rupert's anxious face looking tenderly down at her. She clutched at his hands.

'Oh, Rupert—thank heaven you have come! Pray don't leave me.'

'We appear to be very much *de trop*,' murmured Vivyan, watching this little enactment with a faint, sneering smile.

Hearing his voice, Miss Pensford turned her head.

'Vivyan! I—I think I should tell you. That is—'

'It is quite unnecessary to tell me anything, my dear,' he assured her. 'I quite see how it is, and I am very happy to release you from our understanding.' His glance switched back to Eustacia, who was handing Mr MacCauley a folded napkin for his bloody nose.

'Not everything is quite so clear, however.'

'No, indeed!' retorted Eustacia. 'Perhaps you will tell us why you are here?'

'I came to reclaim my property.' Vivyan glanced at the pistol lying on the table. 'I trust you have its partner safe?'

'It is in my bag. I had hoped you would not notice they were missing quite so soon.'

'I didn't. My groom brought the matter to my attention just after dinner. I take it that was the reason you waylaid me at Kennington Common today?'

'Yes. I hid them in my surcoat. I—I thought I might need them this evening. I was going to return them as soon as I could.'

'After you had used them to commit murder? Thank you.'

'Well now, I did not think it would come to that, but—how did you know where to find me?' She looked accusingly at Rupert. 'I told you in my note to come alone!'

'Oh, don't blame Alleyne. When I realized you had the pistols, I followed you to Addingham House and arrived just as that girl of yours was trying to find a hack. She told me you had driven off with Miss Pensford in a travelling-chaise.'

'Vivyan, you did not bully her?'

'Of course not. She was relieved to tell someone what you had done. And then Alleyne appeared at the door, having received your note from the footman. I—er—persuaded him to let me see it.'

'You see, I had gone to the ball on foot, and Mr Lagallan offered to take me up, there and then, in his chaise,' put in Rupert, somewhat apologetically.

Vivyan's hard eyes were fixed on Eustacia.

'I could have left him to make his own way, of course, but that would have put him some distance behind me, and he would not have had the pleasure of seeing you receive the biggest thrashing of your life.'

Eustacia bit her lip.

'Are you very angry?' she asked, in a small voice.

'Murderously so.'

Mr Alleyne, assured that Miss Pensford was no longer in danger, stepped forward.

'I think, Lagallan, that some of the blame for this evening rests with me. Miss Marchant acted as she did because she believed—she was convinced—that I, that Miss Pensford and I—' He paused, then, drawing himself up, said stiffly, 'If you wish to name your friends, sir—'

'Good God, do you think I want to crown this night's folly with a duel? What I have yet to understand is MacCauley's part in all this.'

Mr MacCauley, who was still nursing his bloody nose, looked up at him over the napkin that was still covering part of his face, but it was Eustacia who spoke.

'Mr MacCauley and I are going to be married!'

The effect of these words was startling. Rupert goggled at her; Mr MacCauley gave a muffled exclamation and tried to rise, but Eustacia thrust him back in his seat. She was very white, but her gaze was steady as she met Vivyan's eyes, noting that all trace of mockery had gone.

Rupert was the first to find his voice.

'Do you mean to tell me you are in love with this . . . this *fellow*?'

'No, dearest, she is not,' said Miss Pensford, sitting up and holding one hand to her head. 'She is marrying him to save her reputation.'

Vivyan was still watching Eustacia, but his glance flickered briefly across to Helen.

'Alleyne, do you think yourself up to the task of conveying Miss Pensford to her home? I think she has endured enough this evening. Take my carriage; I shall make other arrangements.'

'By all means!' declared Mr Alleyne, tenderly helping the lady to her feet.

Vivyan held open the door and, as she passed, Helen put out her hand to him.

'Vivyan, I am sorry—'

He raised her hand to his lips.

'Think no more of it, my dear. I shall call upon your father tomorrow to explain. And take heart, ma'am. I feel sure Alleyne will make you a much better husband.'

He closed the door behind them, and stood gazing across the room at Eustacia, such a brooding look on his face that she was unable to meet his eyes.

'Well, Stacey, I think it is time you explained yourself.'

She tried to look unconcerned.

'There is nothing to explain, sir. I have told you: I am to marry Mr MacCauley.'

'And an elopement was necessary?'

Mr MacCauley looked up again. 'No, I—'

'Yes,' Eustacia interrupted, forcing herself to meet Vivyan's cold gaze. 'I thought it would be exciting. And it gave me the opportunity to end your disastrous engagement to Helen

Pensford.'

'And am I supposed to be grateful for that?'

'Well, I think you should be,' she said, in her frank way. 'Not only is Helen very much in love with Rupert, she is far too respectable for you, and would never make you happy.'

'And that's your reason for running off with MacCauley?'

'No, but it also solves my problem of what to do about Nan and Tom. They will come with us to Dorset. I understand Mr—Nathan's establishment there is quite large, so Tom can be a footman, and we will find Nan work in the kitchens or as a chambermaid.'

A muffled protest from Nathan MacCauley went unnoticed.

'Then what did Helen mean when she said you were marrying MacCauley to save your reputation?'

Again, Mr MacCauley made to rise, and again Eustacia prevented him.

'I do think you would do better to put your head back, and pinch your nose so,' she told him, ignoring Vivyan.

Mr Lagallan watched with growing impatience.

'Well? Do I get an answer, Stacey, or am I to wring it out of you?'

'She was much mistaken,' said Eustacia, not looking at him. 'Hysterical, even.'

'Really?' Vivyan's voice was dangerously calm. 'Let me tell you what I think she meant by it.' He walked forward until only the table separated them, and above the folds of the bloody napkin, Nathan MacCauley's eyes watched him warily.

'I think,' said Mr Lagallan, 'I think that MacCauley threatened to spread the story that you had come to London under my protection.'

Eustacia's sudden blush gave him his answer, although she quickly denied it.

'What nonsense!' she declared, with a derisory laugh. 'I—I have come to know Mr Mac—Nathan—very well, and . . . and I thought it would suit me to marry him. Especially,' she added, as another thought came to her, 'especially since Rupert is in love with Helen.'

'Oh, so you still love Alleyne?'

'No—that is, I—I love Nathan,' she declared, defiantly staring at Vivyan.

Mr MacCauley jumped up.

'Oh no you don't!' he cried. He dabbed cautiously at his nose, which seemed at last to have stopped bleeding. He stepped away from the table, his anxious gaze shifting from Miss Marchant to Vivyan.

'I'll tell you what it is, Lagallan, the girl's out of her senses! In love with me, indeed! You guessed right, Viv, I *did* want to force her to marry me. I wanted to turn respectable, as I told you . . .'

'It seems we all have our dreams, Nathan,'

murmured Vivyan.

'Aye, well, I told her that if she didn't agree to marry me, I would spread it about that she had come to London as your mistress! Well, she wasn't having any of that, so we struck a bargain. But then what must she do but insist I hire a coach and bring it to Addingham House this evening, to collect her and her maid, only when I turn up it ain't no maid at all, but your fiancée whom she bundles into the coach! Then, when the poor girl's crying fit to burst, and I say I'll have nothing to do with a kidnap, she draws out that popgun of yours and sits there as cool as you please, telling me we've to wait for young Alleyne to come and rescue the young woman! Well, I tell you to your head, Viv, I've never seen anything like it, not even when we was in Orleans, and that high-flyer you had taken up with thought you was playing her false!' He looked at Miss Marchant. 'I'll tell you what I'm going to do, Miss, I'm going up to my bed, and you can take the coach back to Town and we'll forget everything that's happened. I want nothing more to do with you!'

Eustacia stared at him.

'What of our agreement?'

'Cancelled!' he declared. 'Finished! Null and void! I want no more to do with a woman who thinks nothing of kidnapping her friends and keeping pops in her pocket! And to cap it all, when I was helping Miss Pensford to lie down, as any Christian gentleman would, what must that young Alleyne do but draw my cork! I tell you, Viv, if those are the ways of the Quality, you may keep 'em! I want nothing more to do with your world!'

The sneering look had vanished from Vivyan's eyes. He laughed.

'Nathan, my friend, I thought you liked a woman with spirit!'

A rueful smile curled MacCauley's lips.

'Aye, but not one that would drive me to Bedlam! I'll leave this one to you, Lagallan, and wish you joy of her!'

'Thank you. I think a spell abroad would suit you best, MacCauley.'

'Aye, even the Frenchies was more civilized than this!' he said, keeping the table between himself and Eustacia as he edged towards the door. 'Maybe I'll take myself off to Dorset to inspect my property. That should be far enough from you all! I bid you goodnight.'

Mr MacCauley slipped out of the room, and Eustacia stared at the door as it closed behind him.

'Well!' she exclaimed, an indignant flush mounting her cheeks. 'How—how ungentlemanly! To go back on an agreement in such a fashion, simply because I wanted a tiny deviation from his plans!'

The amusement in Vivyan's eyes deepened. 'Did you *want* to marry him?'

'Well of course not, but he said if I did not

do so, he would tell everyone how you had brought me to London, which would quite ruin your reputation, and although I did not wish you to marry Helen, I did not want her to cry off because she thought you depraved!'

'But, my dear girl, how on earth did matters reach such a pass? Why did you not come to me?'

She looked away. 'I have imposed upon you far too much already, and I thought that if I told you about MacCauley, you would call him out, which wouldn't solve anything, and he might even have killed you! I—I thought I could resolve it for myself.' She put up her chin. 'And I did just that! Rupert and Helen are happy, you are free, and even Mr MacCauley has decided he does not want to marry me, after all. So you see,' she ended triumphantly, 'there was really no need for you to drive all the way from Town!'

'Oh, I think there was.' He stepped around the table and reached for her hands. 'You have been so busy rescuing everyone else that you have neglected your own case.'

She flushed. 'No, no—I shall take the carriage back to Fanshawe Gardens and invent some tale for Godmama and—and everything will be well.'

'Well, I think I should come with you, and we can inform Lady Bilderston of our engagement.'

Her eyes flew to his face.

'Our—oh, but truly, Vivyan, there is no need—'

He caught her hands, laughing. 'There is *every* need, my adorable little nymph!'

'No, no!' she cried, much distressed. 'I never meant to embroil you in any of this, Vivyan. Please don't feel you have to—*oh!*'

Mr Lagallan put an end to her discourse by the simple expedient of kissing her.

'Oh,' she said again, when at last he released her.

'Before you say anything more, brat, let me tell you that I did not *have* to kiss you, but I *wanted* to. In fact, I have wanted to do that ever since you fell out of that tree and into my arms.'

'You have?' she murmured, nestling happily against him. 'I think I have wanted it, too, for weeks now!'

'So, you think you could put up with me as a husband?'

'It is what I want, more than anything in the world!' She raised her head. 'Oh, but there's Nan and Tom to consider! I promised Nan that she and Tom would come with me to Mr MacCauley's house in the country. Now what am I to do?'

'You must think again, my love. In fact, I think I probably have the solution. Caro is setting up home in Worthing and I will send your precious lovebirds down to her—I am sure she will find work for them.'

'Worthing! Vivyan, you are so clever; that is just the thing. And the sea air will be so beneficial for the baby!'

Bored with the conversation, Vivyan kissed her again, then gently put her away from him.

'I will tell the landlord to prepare your carriage, if we are to get you home before dawn.'

*   *   *

When he came back into the room, he found Miss Marchant standing in the middle of the floor, twisting her hands together, an anxious frown knitting her brow.

'Well, brat, what is it now?' he said, reaching for her again.

She put out her hands against his chest, holding him off.

'Vivyan, are you sure you *truly* want to marry me? I mean—Caroline told me that she did not think you were the type ever to settle down. She said you are addicted to excitement.'

'And so I am, love,' he agreed, his eyes glinting in a way that made her heart race. 'But I think life with you will never be dull, Stacey.'

'Oh, I hope not,' she sighed, melting into his arms again. 'Indeed, I think it will be one long adventure!'